Rarity

by: D.A. Roach

Rarity

Limitless Publishing, LLC
Kailua, HI 96734
www.limitlesspublishing.com

Formatting: Limitless Publishing

ISBN-13: 978-1-68058-172-0
ISBN-10: 1-68058-172-4

Dedication

This book is dedicated to Soren and our vEDS online family. You rock. I hope you all live well into your 80's!

Rarity

Syllabification: rar·i·ty

A thing that is rare, especially one having particular value as a result of this.

(Definition of Rarity courtesy of Oxford Dictionary online.)

Chapter 1

They say empathy is a gift. I never asked for it, and personally, I would've preferred a new car or a vacation in Europe. Like a leech, it slowly sucked the happiness out of me. This particular week was awful. Too many ridiculous and negative customers at the bookstore. But my last shift was hours ago, and as soon as I got home, I went straight to the garden. It was the best way to calm and re-center myself—hands in the dirt. I found myself digging up half the plants in the yard and redesigning the flower beds on a regular basis. Our landscaping looked amazing…Martha Stewart would be proud.

Although there were other empaths in the world, the only other one I'd met was my mom. Without her guidance, I'd be a stressed out and depressed hermit. She helped me find ways to dispel the vampiric energy, and she was trying to teach me how to close myself off to it.

I planted the final zinnia and replaced the stone edging. Then I cleaned my garden tools and hosed off my hands.

"You know, they make garden gloves so you don't get so messy."

I looked up and saw my best friend, Meg—the only teenager I could tolerate being around for extended periods of time. I met Meg in seventh-grade gym class and we meshed instantly. She was short, thin, and awkward, but she was also genuine, kind, and unpretentious. Meg was a little quirky. She always had a stuffed animal with her. In middle school, one would adorn her desk in each class. In high school, she hung small ones off her purse and school bag. It was a quirk I could live with because there was no bullshit about her. She'd been my rock ever since we met, and having her around made everything, including school, more tolerable.

"You know, Meg, a little dirt never hurt anyone. You should try it sometime," I teased.

"Nah. I'll leave the gardening to you, my little white witch."

I turned the hose on Meg. She tried to deflect, but the hose always wins.

"Hey! Enough, enough, truce." We both laughed at what a mess we were.

"Whatcha doin' here?" I asked.

"So, tomorrow is the start of our junior year. Let's celebrate our last night of freedom by having dinner and a movie," Meg suggested.

"Sounds great. I pick the pizza, and you pick the movie?"

"Deal." Meg practically lived at our house, so she knew how to operate our complicated TV set-up. "Brogen, don't you dare put onions on my half."

I smiled back. Of course I wouldn't put the one

topping she hated on the pizza, but she'd have to wait forty-five minutes to find out.

We cleaned up and dried off before we grabbed some drinks and sat on the big, comfy sofa. I wrapped the afghan around me.

"Why do you need a blanket? It's like ninety-five degrees out there, just turn down your air."

"Never, I'd rather be cold with a blanket than sweating. What did you pick?"

She had put in our favorite movie, *Clerks II*. Raunchy, inappropriate, but hysterical.

After the movie, my sides hurt from laughing. "I needed that after my week."

"I bet you're glad to be done with that retail hell you worked this summer," Meg said.

"You have no idea." I took the job at the local bookstore for two reasons—the employee discount, and my Mom thought it'd be good practice on controlling energy. It seemed harmless enough, but…people are people, and most people had very little patience. "I felt so bad for our cashier. This woman was waiting to checkout and was third in line. When it was finally her turn, I could sense her going black…you know, like evil was seeping out of her."

Meg chuckled at my grim description, but the lady was fuming.

I continued. "She said she had called to see if we had a book in stock, and a clerk told her there were twenty copies on hand. But she didn't find it on the shelf."

"So, what, were they all in back?" Meg asked.

"No. We hadn't had any in stock for two weeks.

Poor Jen didn't have a clue what the woman was talking about."

"What the heck was she talking about then?"

"Well, after she left we finally figured out she had called the store across town by accident."

Meg bust out laughing.

"Yeah, it wasn't funny at the time. The woman berated Jen in front of the other customers. Then she left without buying anything and swearing we were a shop of idiots." I shook my head in disgust and disbelief. "It made us look bad, and Jen felt awful."

"Crazy. No wonder you were in the garden." Meg was open enough to understand the emotional toll events like that had on me. She knew just being near people like that would affect me for hours afterward. Empaths found ways to dispel the energy; for me, gardening worked best.

"Are you ready for tomorrow?" Meg asked.

"I guess." Neither of us loved school, but it was a necessary evil. We were our own little clique and steered clear of the big groups. "What about you?"

"Yeah, as ready as I'll ever be."

I glanced at the clock above the TV. 10:30 p.m. "You better get out of here or you'll never wake up on time."

Meg looked at the clock. "Holy cow, ten thirty! I'm outta here. See ya at school, Brogen."

I gave Meg a hug and closed the door after her. Summer had ended, and tomorrow was the start of my junior year.

Chapter 2

Stanton High. It was its own little community within our town. We had geeks, skaters, punks, emos, jocks, preppy kids, gorgeous girls, and a sprinkling of kids who didn't fit any of those descriptions. Meg and I were part of that latter group. Our town was small and the school was nestled in the center of it. Most kids walked or rode their bikes to school, and the few kids who drove their own cars did so to show off their wealth.

Meg found me by my locker. "Well, Brogen, two more years of this place, then we're free." She winked at me before we went our separate ways for our first class.

Mr. Johnson's algebra class held mostly familiar faces. At this stage in our school careers they didn't take the time to announce or introduce the new students. I scanned the room and came across two faces I didn't recognize, a boy and a girl. When Mr. Johnson took roll, I discovered they were Jay Wilken and Becca Grant. Right away it was evident that Becca would fit right in with the gorgeous girl clique. She looked like she spent hours applying makeup and placing each of her golden locks in its perfect position. Jay was harder to place. He was lean, tall, and not overly muscular. Although he was fit, he was probably not a jock. He wore jeans and a t-shirt, which could put him in several groups. His hair was a little messy, ruling out preppy and geek, but not messy enough for skater or emo. But probably too cool to migrate to the small group Meg and I were in. In other words, I had no clue.

Because of my "gift," I was initially very intrigued by people and tried to tune into their energies. Once I figured them out, I'd often find their energy overbearing or negative and would choose to avoid them. So, Jay was a puzzle. And I had a feeling my curiosity would preoccupy my thoughts.

Mr. Johnson passed out our syllabus and said most of the learning would be online this year. Maybe he had a salary cut, or maybe he was getting too old to care about actually teaching us anything. When the period ended, he dismissed us with no homework—at least that was a bonus.

After three more classes, it was lunch time. I sat at the table Meg and I claimed last year. There were four or five others who sat there, but we never intermixed with them. Meg dropped her tray on the table next to me. I looked at it in disgust.

"How can you eat that stuff? What is it anyway...turkey surprise?" I giggled while pinching my nose. "Surprise, there's no turkey in it."

"Shut up. Someone kept me out late last night,

and I was too tired to pack something edible. If I don't eat something, I'll sleep through my last three classes. Besides, I think I see a piece of carrot in there...or wait..." She pushed the food back and forth with her fork. "Never mind, I don't know what that was."

I laughed at Meg's pathetic lunch. "At least I can pinch you awake in two of those classes."

"No joke. Finally. I can't believe we endured freshman and sophomore year without any classes together," Meg said. "Oh hey, did you see the new kid over there?" Meg pointed at Jay, the kid from my algebra class. He sat at a circular table across the room and seemed quite chummy with one of the nicer kids at Stanton, Soren Michaels.

"Yeah, I had him in first period. I think his name is Jay. Do you know anything about him?"

"He was in my chemistry class last period. He seemed pretty nice. Funny, actually. I overheard him say that he was Soren's cousin. Anyway, cute, right?" Meg stared across the lunch room with a dreamy look on her face, and I couldn't help but chuckle.

I studied Jay for a few moments. He had an exotic model look—big eyes, straight dark hair, strong features. I guess he was pretty attractive. He looked up and caught my eye at that moment. His mouth twisted into a half smile and I felt myself blushing. Surely he wasn't directing that smile my way. I turned away and refocused. "Meg, I think it's the new shiny toy effect. Just because it's new doesn't make it more awesome than the other toys."

"Your loss...more for me."

I peered over at his table again. He was still looking in my direction. I checked behind me but there was only a wall. When I turned back I saw he was enthralled in something Soren had said.

"God, wouldn't that suck? Changing schools junior year." I shook my head in astonishment. "I wouldn't want to do that." Jay stood up from the table and put his lunch tray away. I wondered out loud, "Which clique do you think will absorb him?"

"Whatever. Clique-schmick. Just appreciate the attractive specimen added to our little fish bowl." Meg gave me a nudge and grinned.

***

After lunch we finished our day. It was so nice having Meg in my classes, but I was bummed that I had homework on the one night this month my mom didn't have evening patients.

I walked up our front steps and unlocked the front door. The aromas that filled the house made my stomach growl. Mom was making some of her famous lasagna and was busy putting a salad together.

"How'd school go?" she asked.

"It was uninteresting. I hate that they give us homework on the first day. We haven't even learned anything yet."

"That does seem unfair. Do you have a lot to do?"

"No, but it's the principle of it that bugs me."

"Yes, it's probably just to warm you up for the mountain of work they plan to assign," Mom teased.

"Ha ha, funny."

"Seriously, though, everything else went okay?" Having a psychologist as a mom made me wonder if she was in doctor mode or mom mode.

"Fine. The day was pretty uneventful." Even though my mom was empathic like me, she could turn it on and off. She would never be able to work as a psychologist without that ability…being around all those raw emotions of her patients would drain her. She had sympathy for me because she wasn't always able to turn it off, and she remembers how dark the days could be when you absorbed someone's negativity or emotional pain.

"Good. Are you doing your exercises?" she asked.

"Yeah, Mom, every day. I'll do them after supper." Mom said being strong on the inside and outside helped her have more control as an empath. Hopefully it would work for me, and one day I could stop avoiding situations that were too draining for me.

After dinner and cleaning dishes, I changed into my workout clothes and finished my English Lit homework. Then I grabbed a candle and sat on the floor to start meditating. I wasn't into magic, though an outsider might wonder. The candle helped me focus. As I stared at it, I steadied my breathing and tried to slow my heart rate. Each breath leaving and entering my body released some of the tension I'd been holding. Each breath freed my mind of the thoughts cluttering my head. After twenty minutes, my phone alarm chimed. I blew out the candle and stretched in preparation for my run. I tied my laces and put in my earbuds before heading out the door.

I ran at least five days a week, and I ran until my mind was free from the day. I usually kept a steady pace until I felt the calm of nothingness take over, then I would sprint home to get my heart rate up. Running at dusk was the time I enjoyed most; everything seemed so peaceful. The sun was setting, painting the sky with various colors now that the heat of the day was gone.

After my run, I waved as I passed Mom in the living room. She seemed more at ease lately. Time had healed her wounds. My father's affair destroyed our family, and although I hated being without both parents, I hated my father's selfishness and what it did to my mom even more. I jogged up the wood steps, grabbed my pjs, and then hit the shower.

Before bed, I started my last daily ritual—I drew in my art journal. Since the divorce, I began sketching nightly, and I promised myself I would not look back at the pages until I filled the book, cover to cover. I dated the top corner of the page and got out my pencil. I never paid much attention to what I drew; usually, there were some pictures and words on a page that resembled what I felt inside. Once I finished drawing, I stashed the sketchbook under my nightstand and grabbed my new novel. Before I knew it, I felt my mom kiss my forehead and set my book down while whispering, "Goodnight."

Chapter 3

After the first week of school, Becca had officially become the leader of the gorgeous girls' clique, aka the Blonde-squad, and she was quickly showing she was not the sweet, innocent girl she first appeared to be. I overheard some of the football players in the hall behind me. "Did you see how she was licking that lollipop? I'd like to have her lick *my* lollipop." Eye roll. Did all high school guys think with their dicks? They could have her. I didn't want some shallow guy like that as a boyfriend. They'd probably end up cheating on their women, like my dad did.

Jay was still a mystery to me, but I did know about his cousin, Soren. He was a likable guy who joked around with people in all groups and never seemed to get in the mix of any conflict. He ran track and seemed smart. Too bad he wasn't my type. His dark curly hair, olive skin, and short stature were polar opposites of my preferences. I was attracted to tall and trim guys, kind of like Jay. Today, Jay wore a Def Leppard t-shirt with his

11

worn jeans. Def Leppard was old school, but cool, and Jay made that tee and jeans look amazing. What the heck was I doing? I couldn't think like that. We were in different leagues. He's gorgeous *and* the new shiny thing. Every girl wanted him, including Meg, but it would probably be someone like Becca who landed him. She had the looks and the social standing.

It was impossible to focus in algebra, what with Jay only three rows away. Each day I grew more intrigued, and each day I became more attracted to him…yet I was no closer to uncovering where he fit in. He was a chameleon, forever blending and changing to match his environment. Halfway through class, I noticed Jay was looking at Becca, studying her. He had to be attracted to her; she was beautiful and popular. It was only a matter of time before he made his move on her.

"Brogen. Brogen Mathers? Please tell us the answer to number five."

Oh, crud. I snapped out of my daydream and saw Jay looking at me with a half smile. *Busted*. I'd been staring in his direction while Mr. Johnson called me out. I sat straighter and scanned my paper. "Umm, thirty-seven."

"Correct. Please try to remain focused for the rest of class," he chided me.

I felt my cheeks pink up and wished I could hide under a rock. Becca snickered at me, officially placing her on my "People I Love to Hate" list. The bell couldn't ring soon enough. I grabbed my things and walked to my locker. I plunked my head on the locker door, needing a moment of solitude. I hated being caught in embarrassing moments. I liked to fly under the radar, and being embarrassed in front of Jay made it worse.

"Excuse me." I heard a guy's voice behind me.

I turned around, not sure who to expect. Jay stood in front of me and my heart began pounding rapidly in my chest. Why was he here? What did he want? Maybe he was confronting me for staring at him? Maybe he wanted to heckle me like Becca? Maybe he mistook me for someone else?

"You left this on your desk." He held out my phone.

"Thanks. That would have cost way too much to replace." I couldn't look him in the eye. My hands trembled, and my stomach flip-flopped as I reached for the phone. Why was my treacherous body reacting like this to the new boy toy?

"No problem. I'm Jay, by the way."

"Brogen. But you probably knew that after Mr. Johnson called on me several times." I decided to be brave and look up. It was only polite, after all. But the second our eyes met, he smiled, and I knew I was in trouble. He was beautiful.

"Yeah, Brogen, got it. Anyway, see ya."

"Thanks again," I managed.

Jay waved and headed down the hall while I stared after him in awe. Ugh, my crazy teenage-girl hormones were spinning out of control.

"Spill it." I jumped nearly fifty feet at the sound of Meg's voice.

"Crap, you scared me to death!"

"Yeah, kinda funny 'cause I wasn't even trying. So, what did the new guy want?"

Jay turned back for one last glance in my direction before rounding the corner. I let out a long sigh. Turning to Meg, I gave her a level look. "It seems I left my brains in my last class." Her eyebrows raised in disbelief. "Actually, I spaced in algebra and left my phone in class. He was just nice enough to return it."

She stuck her pointer finger in my chest. "You like him. When's the hot date?"

"Ugh. What am I gonna do with you?"

"Love me." She grinned.

"I already do."

The rest of the day went by quickly, probably because my mind kept wandering to thoughts about Jay. He was so likable and confident, almost unbelievable. After the last period, Meg met me at my locker so we could leave together.

"I don't get it. How are these new kids coming in and ruling the school?" I pondered. "I mean, Jay…he should be struggling to fit in. It takes years to advance social ranks, but he's befriended the whole school in the first week."

"Charisma and hot bods, my friend," Meg replied.

"And Becca. She went straight to number one on day one," I complained.

"Charisma and hot bods again, my friend."

I stopped to glare at her, but maybe she was right. Meg turned down her street and I continued my walk home. I slowed my pace when I saw the dark green Saab in the driveway. My dad's car. I hadn't seen him in years and had no desire to see him now. I walked up the steps and quietly entered the front door. Rather than hollering out, "Hi, Mom," I listened and approached cautiously, like a cat stalking its prey. I slid off my backpack and crept toward the kitchen. I heard two voices— Mom's and Dad's.

"I wanna see her more," he said.

"Why now? What selfish reason is behind all of this? Are you trying to impress your new bed buddy?" Mom was mad. I was grateful she was reluctant to throw me back into my dad's arms.

"No. Is it a crime to want to see my daughter? I don't think so."

"No, but it's a crime to destroy our family and stay away for more than five years. I don't want your help now, I don't need it, and I am not sure your daughter is ready for you to come parading back into her life. But that is her own decision. I cannot speak for her."

"God. You are so frustrating. No wonder I left you." That last part was mumbled, but Mom and I both heard it. Ouch.

"Get out. Get out now!" I hid behind the upholstered chair and heard my dad mutter something about lawyers and papers. Then, the door slammed, and my mom let out a huge sigh and hit her fist on the door.

"Hey, Mom. You okay?"

I must have scared the life out of her, because she jumped and let out a small scream. "I didn't know you were home. When did you get in?" She looked from me and back to the door where my dad had just left.

"Long enough to hear you both argue. You

okay?"

"I will be. His visit caught me off guard. I mean, we haven't heard from him in years…" She sighed again, clearly trying to let go of the tension that built up from their argument.

"Maybe *you* need a run?"

She laughed and smiled. "Thanks, *mom*, I think I'll do that." She gave me a big hug and went upstairs to change into workout clothes. "I won't be long, and supper is cooking in the oven."

At dinner that night, I asked my mom why my dad had stopped by earlier. She truly seemed surprised to have seen him.

"He says he wants more time with you. But why now? I just don't get it." I didn't know either, and I felt uncomfortable at the thought of trying to rebuild a relationship with someone I didn't care for anymore. She pushed her food around her plate, clearly still upset. "Change of subject…how's school?"

"Ahh, not much happens the first week." *There's a gorgeous guy at our school, and I can't get a read on him, which makes him occupy my thoughts even more…* "I'm glad I have Meg in a few classes this year."

"I like Meg. She's so good for you." I nodded in agreement. "Are you going on a run after dinner?" Mom asked.

"Yep. I'll help with some dishes first since my food has to settle."

"Just some?" She winked at me. "Guess I should take what I can get."

With the dishes done, I pulled my hair into a

ponytail and put on my workout clothes. It was still warm from the late summer air, so I wore my tank runner top and knee-length stretch pants. I tied my laces, strapped on my phone, and stretched on the front porch. I didn't run yesterday and had a lot on my mind today—Jay and Dad. I felt like a bottle of soda being shaken, ready to burst. The run would let some of that pressure escape.

I took off toward the school. There was a large soccer field nearby where I could run laps before sprinting home. On my run, I kept replaying the Jay interaction over and over again. When that would stop, I heard my dad and mom arguing. I ran faster. I didn't want to run all night long and hoped the increased speed would clear my mind faster as well. I focused on my breathing and the burn in my upper thighs. Before I knew it, I had run five laps around the soccer field and was headed home. Unfortunately, the sun had gone down and the streetlamps were the only light source illuminating my path. I felt the numbing calm from deep within begin to wash the day's worries away. I was on autopilot...until I saw two glowing eyes right in front of me and heard the bone-chilling snarl.

I froze as the dog stalked into the light. He didn't look like my neighbor's friendly pup. His hair was clumped together, his eyes wild. When he bared his teeth, a froth of white saliva dripped to the street. Where the hell had this dog come from? Fear trickled down my spine as I debated my course of action. Run as fast and hard as I could—home was just a few blocks away—or stand my ground and not act scared. Someone once told me dogs could sense your fear…I was screwed. His eyes tracked me. My heart was thundering in my chest. The adrenaline from the run mixed with fear would probably give me a heart attack if I couldn't calm down. Each growl made my muscles tense in anticipation of his attack. Okay, having trouble calming down…the only thing left to do was to make a run for it. I scanned ahead for my best route. I needed obstacles because this pooch could likely outrun me. As I glanced to my left, a loud clatter came from close by. The dog and I turned to the noise. There was someone standing in the shadows of a nearby tree. I couldn't see who it was, so I took advantage of the distraction and started running. I heard the claws clicking on the pavement as the dog moved toward one of us. I didn't dare look.

I heard a scuffle behind me. A guy shouted at the dog and cursed as if he were in pain. Jesus, that dog was probably making a meal of him. I knew I needed to keep running, but found my feet had stopped and turned to face the melee. I saw a body curled on the street, the person shielding their face. The dog approached. I needed to help. I searched for a rock or stick to defend myself. I found a dead branch on an oak and began trying to crack it off the trunk. As I gave one last tug, I heard the squeal of tires, a high pitched yelp, and a thud. I turned to see a car stopped in the road. Rust-colored streaks coated the headlights that illuminated the motionless dog lying a few feet away. Oh crap, what about the guy who distracted the dog? Did the driver hit him? I ran to the car and looked around. The driver was bent over, checking on the person lying on the ground. It was hard to see very well since the only light came from the streetlamps and the blood-streaked headlights. I stepped closer. Blood everywhere. Tears formed in my eyes, and I was afraid the person in the road was dead. The driver was talking to the person, slurring his words and clearly intoxicated. His body moved.

"Oh man, are you okay?" I asked.

He rolled over and faced me. I was looking into the gorgeous eyes of Jay.

"Jay! Oh crap, you need to get to a hospital." I un-cuffed my phone and began dialing with shaking hands. He was a mess. There was lots of blood, but it mostly looked dog inflicted. I gave the 911 operator our location and fought back the tears. I gently moved my hand around his body to assess the damage. "You saved me. But look at you…" I shook my head. I needed to get Jay to focus on me and stay alert. "I'm glad you were wearing jeans. It gave a little more barrier to the dog's teeth." I scanned his body while talking to 911. "They wanna know if you were you hit by the car," I asked quietly, not wanting to engage the drunk man, who was now pacing the scene of the accident. Jay shook his head. I finished giving details to the operator and then crouched next to Jay.

He gave me a wry smile. "Brogen, I need you to go down the street to my house. Tell my aunt I got hurt. 726, house number is near the front door."

"I don't wanna leave you."

"I'm not goin' anywhere. And it will be a few minutes till the ambulance gets here. I'll be fine. Please," he begged.

"Okay, stay put, and don't die on me." He chuckled at my doom and gloom comment. I ran down the street and found the house Jay mentioned. I rang the bell, and it felt like twenty minutes had passed before someone answered the door.

"Yes?" asked an older, beautiful woman.

"Hi, I need you to come with me *now*. Your nephew Jay is down the street. He's been hurt. An ambulance is on the way."

"An ambulance?" Her face contoured with worry, and she swiftly slipped her shoes on. She followed me to where Jay lay. Tears were falling down her face. "What happened?" She reached out and took Jay's hand.

"A dog came out of nowhere and attacked," Jay said. He was looking a bit pale. I listened hard for the ambulance and could swear I heard it in the distance.

"Jay saved me. And this guy," I pointed to the inebriated man pacing around his car, "came around the corner and hit the dog." I looked back at Jay and said, "You're pretty lucky he didn't run you over. And thank you again for saving me."

"Anything for a babe in distress." He smiled at me and winked.

I couldn't hold back my small chuckle. "Even if it means becoming Cujo's chew toy?"

I heard the car door open and saw the drunk man getting in his car. Was he trying to leave the scene of the accident?

The ambulance pulled up behind his car, thankfully making a quick getaway impossible. Jay was quickly evaluated for broken bones or sprains.

The EMTs commented on how he had several bite wounds and a lot of blood loss. They also mentioned something about a rabies shot. It all went so fast, maybe from shock setting in, or maybe they whisked him off because of the severity of his injuries. Jay left in the ambulance, and his aunt followed in her car.

"Excuse me, can we get a quick statement from you, ma'am?" There was a tall, chubby police officer standing next to me with a notepad in his hand. I'd been too busy focusing on Jay to even notice the cops had arrived. The other officer was questioning the driver and asking him to walk a straight line. I gave a rundown of events to the cop. He offered to drive me home, but I thought the walk would help. I didn't live far from there.

Jay had saved me. He was so bloody, so wounded. The image would haunt my dreams. The drunk driver saved us from that rabid dog, and I couldn't believe I was thankful for a drunk driver coming to the rescue. That was all kinds of wrong. But had he not turned down the street when he did, Jay and I might have met a different fate. The whole night seemed surreal.

Once inside, my mom shouted a greeting to me from the kitchen. I took off my shoes and headed in for some water. Mom was unloading the dishwasher. She turned toward me, and dropped the platter that was in her hands. It smashed into jagged pieces all over the floor.

"Damnit!" she said, looking at the floor a quick second, then turned her focus back to me. "What in the world happened to you? Are you okay?"

"I'm okay. A little shook up, though."

"My goodness, you were gone so long, I almost went looking for you." A strand of hair fell out of my ponytail, and she tucked it behind my ear. "You look awful. What happened?" She took a step back to get a better look at me. "Is that blood on your hands? Are you hurt? Sit down." I sat obediently and felt tremors rising to the surface. "Drink some water." I drank, but the glass made a clanging sound as my trembling hands tried to place it down. "Listen, I need to know if you are hurt."

"I'm not. I'm okay. But he's hurt. He risked his life for me." The last part of that sentence was so quiet it sounded like a breath.

"Who? What the hell happened?"

I felt cold tingles up and down my arm and across my chest. I felt panic and adrenaline mixing together to form a potent cocktail in my blood. And then, everything went black.

Chapter 4

The next morning I awoke to the most delicious smell...bacon. I sat up and saw the light of the new day filtered through my sheer drapes. Everything was so quiet and peaceful. I lay there a few extra minutes, appreciating the softness of my comforter wrapped around me. When I heard dishes clanging, I grabbed my robe and made my way downstairs. Mom was humming a tune while tending the stove.

"Hey, Mom."

"Hey. You're awake. How are you feeling?" she asked.

"Like I was struck by lightning yesterday...fizzled out."

"That's to be expected. Take it easy today, and be sure to get out for a walk. Maybe later you can tell me what happened last night, but first, time for breakfast."

I loved that my mom wasn't pushy. She knew I needed time to breathe and not relive the events from last night. I wondered if Jay made it home last night or if he had to stay at the hospital. I shook the

23

thought away as I felt my heart rate picking up. I took some very slow and discrete breaths so my mom wouldn't notice. Then, I focused on the amazing plate of morning yums in front of me.

"This looks delicious. I love your Saturday morning breakfasts, Mom."

She leaned forward and kissed my forehead. "You're welcome. I like them too."

After cleaning up the breakfast items, I took a long and hot shower. I had no plans for the day since I didn't feel well from yesterday's events. I put on my sweats and an old t-shirt, and then snuggled with a blanket on the couch while watching movies. At lunch, Mom brought home Chinese food and began asking me about last night.

As I recounted my interaction with the dog, she looked terrified. Her face matched the feelings I had last night. I went on to explain Jay and the dog's struggle, and finally the drunk driver who "saved the day."

"Well, first off, I'm glad you are okay and feel grateful this Jay jumped in to help you. How did he end up being there at the right time?" She studied me. I shrugged and shook my head because I couldn't explain it. I guess it was fate. Mom continued, "I mean, that's fortuitous." I nodded in agreement. I flashed back to Jay laying in the street looking very bloody. Mom's voice began again, "Well, do you recall much about coming home last night?"

"Honestly, no. All I remember was thinking I could just walk home instead of catch a ride with a cop, but then it seemed like it took two hours to walk a couple of blocks."

"Well, my dear Brogen, you had a full-on panic attack last night. You came in clearly upset, blood on your hands, and began trembling and breathing fast. Before I knew it, you passed out from hyperventilating. I got you conscious enough to help you to your room. That's why you feel so 'frizzled.' After effects of the adrenaline from yesterday."

"Crazy. That sounds vaguely familiar, the shaking hands I mean. Could it happen again? Is it a one-time deal or what?"

"I hope it's a one-time thing. But listen, if you start feeling like your heart is racing, you need to get someplace where you can calm down and breathe it out. It takes a single thought to send you into a panic attack and start the adrenaline cycle, but it takes fifteen minutes for the adrenaline to subside. You need to get calm in those fifteen minutes. Breathing helps the most." I nodded in understanding. "Anything else you want to tell me?"

I thought for a second. "I'm worried about Jay. I'm sure he'll be in school Monday and I can check in with him then, but it's hard to not know how he is."

Mom reached over and gave me a big hug. "I'm sure he's fine."

Mom cleaned up our lunch, and I excused myself to the bathroom. When I finished, I saw Meg standing in the kitchen with my mom, speaking in a quiet voice to her.

"I can hear you." I lied and heard them resume

their quiet words. My mom was probably filling Meg in on last night's events.

"So, Jay to the rescue. Lucky you. Are you gonna get a bat signal installed with the letter J on it?" Meg said jokingly.

"Har har, very funny…not. Seriously, he got pretty mangled. Did you hear a drunk driver saved us by hitting the dog? He totally saved our lives. It's unreal." I sat on the bench in the front hall, lacing up my shoes. "No run today, I feel like garbage. Just a walk." Meg smiled and nodded. She wasn't super athletic, so she preferred a walk to a run.

"Glad you're okay and Jay spared you from becoming that dogs next meal. Boys look cute in scars, girls don't." There was a lot more meaning coming off of Meg that she didn't say. She was truly grateful I was alive and okay. I hugged her before we went out the door.

"I'd like to walk past his place and see if his aunt's car is there. I'm dying to know if he made it home last night or if he had to stay at the hospital." Meg and I started down the street and paused when we came to the intersection where all of last night's action happened. "Look at that, still some blood left on the road from the dog. And tire marks from the driver trying to stop."

Meg walked around the area. "Boy, you both are lucky you didn't get hit by the car."

"I know." I peered down the street, but I didn't see any vehicle at Jay's aunt's house. "Anyway, let's head home."

***

On Monday, I didn't see Jay anywhere. I searched his lunch table and saw Soren sitting there with his buddies. He looked over and acknowledged me with a nod. I had to know if Jay was okay, but I didn't have the nerve to approach Soren with all those people around. I floated through my day, stewing over why Jay was there when the dog attacked and why he wasn't at school today. I'd have to actually read my textbooks to find out what my teachers were talking about because my brain was elsewhere. The final bell rang, and I packed up my homework and headed out the school doors. I saw Soren finishing up with one of his track buddies and decided to slow my steps in hopes to chat with him alone.

"Hey, Soren, got a second?" I asked.

"Hey, Brogen, how are you?" He looked me up and down—not in a sexual 'checking you out' kinda way, but in a 'do you have any noticeable injuries' kinda way.

"I'm better. No outward scars. Not sure about the internal scarring yet. That whole night was a mess. Where's Jay? He wasn't at school today."

"He's better. He got released from the hospital Sunday morning. He'll have a lot of scars…I think they said sixty-five stitches in total, plus rabies shots. My mom thought he should take it easy today and have a relaxing day at home. He'll be back tomorrow"

My head fell into my hands and shook in disbelief. I couldn't help feeling like it was my fault, though I did nothing to precipitate this event. "Thanks for the update. There was a lot of blood…were his bites deep?"

"All the bites were about the same…medium severity. Jay has a way of getting a little more hurt than most people. I mean, as kids, we could all jump off the same table and scuff our knees, but Jay would always require a hospital visit, stitches, or glue. Just unlucky, I guess."

"Well, I'm really grateful he helped me. I'll thank him the next time I see him. Please tell him I said hello."

"Hey, are you sure you're okay? Jay was asking me to check in with you. Honestly, I almost forgot, so I'm glad you approached me. He was really worried about you."

I couldn't believe he was worried about me. I didn't even get a scratch. I was starting to see some of his charm. "Tell him I'm good and that I hope he feels better."

"Okay. See ya, Brogen."

I waved goodbye and started on my way home. Meg caught up with me and asked about my chat with Soren.

"Wow, Jay was asking about you. Nice," she said.

I nodded in agreement. Soren and Jay were both pretty great guys in my book. And Jay was going to be back at school in the morning.

Chapter 5

The next day, Jay walked into algebra wearing jeans and a long sleeved t-shirt. No bandages or stitches visible. He caught me looking at him and gave me a little smile. I smiled back, blushed, and looked down at my paper in embarrassment. I wasn't brave enough to look at him any more in class, but I could swear he glanced at me several times. When the bell rang, I gathered my books and quickly exited the class, too bashful to talk to him. Clearly he was okay. He was at school, after all. What more did I need to ask him?

I went to my locker and traded out my books for my next class. I heard Becca's sickly sweet sing-song voice and couldn't help but see who she was targeting. Coming around the corner, I saw her long blonde hair bouncing before I saw the rest of her, and then I saw him. Jay. Becca had her arms wrapped around him, and she was praising him for being so heroic. My heart dropped. I liked Jay, probably more than I cared to admit to myself, and now the Blonde-squad's leader was weaving her web around him. He had no chance. He didn't look amused. His face actually seemed like he was barely tolerating her. But all it would take was a tight shirt, an earful of compliments, and lots of touching to sway him to loving her. She was beautiful, and he was a teenage boy with raging hormones.

Jay had scored many points in my book with the dog fiasco, but this took half of those away. It wasn't because I liked him any less. I just saw him as less attainable, less worth pursuing. I hurried away, not wanting to show my disappointment to him. Another school day lost to Jay on the brain. At this rate I'd have to repeat my junior year.

Lunch time finally came around and Meg sat next to me. "What's with the funk?"

"Becca. She's making her move on Jay. It's painful to watch."

"Ugh, gross. Is he falling for it?" she asked.

"It's only a matter of time. I need to just thank him and bury my thoughts of him."

"Boy, you really had it for him." She took a bite of her sandwich and looked over at Jay's table. "That's too bad. He's cute and funny. You'd be cute together."

"Not gonna happen…" I trailed off when suddenly Meg's eyes opened wide and she was staring up above my head. "What?" I turned in my chair and saw a torso, with jeans and a long sleeve t-shirt. I looked higher and saw Jay smiling down at me.

"Hey, mind if I sit here for a minute?" he asked.

I couldn't speak. I was in shock. He publicly

acknowledged me and wanted to sit next to me in the lunch room. I nodded, though I doubt he would have taken no for an answer.

"Brogen, I wanted to see if you were okay."

Meg kept stomping on my foot in excitement. "Yeah, I'm fine. Soren asked me yesterday. How are you?" I gave Meg a dirty look to try and get her to stop abusing my foot.

"Ah, believe it or not, I'm used to emergency rooms. The bites will heal. The shots sucked. But, the plus side is I get out of gym for the week *and* I got to talk to you." I raised my eyebrows in disbelief over that last phrase.

"Hell of a way to meet someone," Meg added.

Jay studied my face. "You seemed pretty shook up that night. Every time I closed my eyes these last two days, I would see that scared look on your face. It haunted me."

"Well, I *was* pretty scared. I don't know how or why you showed up when you did, but I'm so grateful."

He smiled at me and I felt my heartbeat quicken. "Fate, I guess. My aunt asked me to put a letter in the mailbox. I headed down the driveway and heard some growling. I came closer and saw you and that angry-looking dog. I wish I had a different game plan, but I was worried it might attack you. I tried to distract it. Guess it worked."

"Well, thank you. I wish you hadn't been hurt, though. Have you heard anything about that drunk driver?"

"Yeah, my aunt followed up with the cops. They gave him a fine and he has to take some driving classes. They let him off easy because he saved us. Can you believe that?"

I shook my head. "Is he really not going to drive drunk again? I mean, that's not much of a punishment. He could have hit you."

"Yeah, I don't know."

Soren approached the table and put a hand on Jay's shoulder. "Hey, Brogen. Hey, Meg...ready to go, Jay?"

Meg and I looked at each other. It was as if Stanton High had been transported into the *Twilight Zone*. Meg and I were shadows at school. We didn't stand out or interact with many other students. This whole Soren and Jay thing was changing our world.

"Yeah. Anyway, Brogen, I'm glad you're okay." Jay stood and gently touched my shoulder as he walked away. Meg and I needed a moment to close our mouths and collect ourselves.

"What the heck?" Meg said.

I shrugged my shoulders. I had no words for what just happened. Now that I'd thanked him, could I really ignore him from now on? The rest of the day, I replayed our interaction at lunch and fought with Meg as she teased me for spacing out.

At the end of the day, I saw the Blonde-squad surrounding Becca. One of them pointed in my direction, and suddenly, all eyes fell on me. What the hell? Why were they pointing at me? I hurried at my locker so I could get home fast. As I walked past, I heard Becca's voice mutter "loser." What the heck? What was her beef with me?

"Why are we speed-walking?" I turned and saw Meg next to me, trying to keep up.

"Avoiding the Blonde-squad," I muttered.

"Oh? Why are you avoiding them? Are they trying to absorb you into their superficial blonde-hood?"

I stopped and laughed. Oh, how I loved my best friend. "No, Meg, I don't think they are eager to let me in to their little circle. Becca was hanging all over Jay after algebra this morning. Then she and her followers were staring me down at my locker. I don't want her brand of drama."

"Huh, so she sees you as a threat. That's not good. Not good for Jay, and especially not good for you. She's going to target you and do whatever she can to make you less appealing to Jay, and probably make your life a living hell."

"I'm already *not* appealing to Jay. He was just checking on me," I argued.

"You are *too* appealing to him. He saved you. That creates a special bond between you two. You survived a stressful situation together and helped each other. You can't buy that in a bottle."

She was right. I felt that bond grow between Jay and me that night. "Shit. I'm in trouble." Meg puffed out her cheeks and nodded.

When my mom got home from seeing patients that night, I told her about the events of the day. "Mom, I'm worried this Becca is gonna start some drama."

"Well, they haven't really done anything yet. People will say what they want and can be cruel. It's up to us to decide whether we let their words in to hurt us. You just have to decide to not let it in. Maybe she'll give up once she realizes it's not affecting you. Don't give her words any power."

It was worth a try. I mean, my mom went through lots of school and has helped many people improve their relationships with others, surely she'd be spot on with her advice.

The week continued very much like that Tuesday had. Jay would purposely bump into me at my locker, smile, and say, "Oh, sorry, excuse me." I'd blush, despite my efforts to not be affected by him. On Friday, he joined our lunch table at the end of the period to "update me on his healing progress." Meg and I think he deliberately left his hoodie so I'd have to seek him out to return it. All the while, Becca was putting forward an excellent effort to ensnare Jay. She tried to burn my skin with her venomous glare during the two classes I had with her, and I did my best to ignore, just as mom suggested.

I continued with my drawing and meditation after dinner. I moved my running time to after school, hoping to avoid the after-work bar hoppers. I needed to be strong, physically and mentally, in case the Blonde-squad attacked. School was in full swing, and there were talks of the upcoming Homecoming dance and tryouts for several winter sports. The high school melodrama was in the air, you could almost smell it—sickly sweet at times, rancid and putrid the rest of the time.

In Tuesday's art club, Meg teased, "Are you going out for basketball this year?" She knew I didn't do organized team sports.

"Nah, too busy trying to become a world class artist," I teased back. Meg and I joined art club because it looked good on college applications, was fun, and the people in there were easy to like and get along with.

"I heard Jay went out for swimming and made the team," Meg said while looking at me curiously for a response. I nodded my head. "Wonder what he looks like in a swimsuit?" I turned and tapped her hand with my paint-soaked paintbrush. "Hey, just sayin'." She snickered as she walked away to wash off the paint.

In algebra, I was treated to a sick display of Becca in all her glory. She had on a very tight, low-cut white shirt and a flowy miniskirt. She kept giggling and writing notes, then passed them to Jay. I felt like gagging. He blushed a few times, chuckled a little, and then wrote back and passed it to her. I couldn't believe my eyes. I guess the stressful event bond we had was wearing off. I didn't want to watch them, but I couldn't help it. I wondered what was on those papers, but knew I would never find out.

I was pissed off and jealous. My mood was spoiled for the day. I slammed my locker, avoided all eye contact, and I didn't even look Jay's way at lunch. Meg could tell something was up, but she didn't mess with me. She knew I needed space. He was out of my league. He could have any girl. I was dreaming big and needed a big fat reality pinch. *Wake the hell up.* Before the day was out, the Blonde-squad dropped another "loser" on me. And Jay "accidentally" bumped into me while walking— not once, but twice. I didn't look up either time. I didn't acknowledge him. I was glad it was Friday so

I could re-center and be away from the drama of high school.

At dinner that night, Mom told me my dad wanted to take me to dinner on Saturday.

"Why is he trying to have a relationship with me now? I don't get it. I'm almost an adult. He missed a huge chunk of my life. I don't need him now." This day felt like that book *Alexander and the Terrible, Horrible, No Good, Very Bad Day.*

"I don't know, sweetie. My guess is he has a new girl he's trying to impress, one with kids of her own, and he's trying to make a good impression. Or, maybe he was too selfish to help raise you, but now that you are self-sufficient, he wants back in. Or maybe he doesn't want to pay child support anymore." Mom was grasping at straws. None of her reasons included him getting to know me because he missed me. "Maybe you'll get a better feel of things after the dinner."

"Why are you okay with this?" I asked.

"I'm not, sweetie, but a court battle can be costly and ugly. I guess I'm hoping you both either realize it's okay to have a relationship or that it's not, and we can move on," she admitted.

Saturday evening came quick, and I dressed in a skater style short dress with black leggings. My dad rang our bell and told my mom he'd have me back after dinner. He seemed older and shorter than I remembered. He still had a full head of hair and was fairly attractive for a middle-aged guy. As I walked down the driveway I could make out two other people already in the car. I got in the backseat.

My dad sat in front and turned to face me.

"Brogen, this is Becca and her mom, Linda Grant. They will be joining us for dinner."

I turned to greet the girl in the backseat with me and it was Becca from *school*. Oh my God. I wanted to exit the car and go back inside. Now I had to be cordial to her and her mom? This night was sucking more by the second. I painted on the best fake smile I could. Screw my life.

"How do you know them?" I asked.

"Linda and I work together across town, and her daughter, Becca, goes to your school. Have you met before?"

"Not formally," I replied. I turned to Becca and tried to look as carefree as possible. "Nice to meet you, Becca." She returned the fake smile and shook my hand.

"Linda and I started dating a few weeks ago, and we thought it might be a nice opportunity for you all to meet. They're new in town."

How incredibly sweet of you father. I've barely seen you in the last years of my life, and you pull me into your new relationship with the newest Blonde-squad's member. Just let me make it through the night.

"We have reservations at Maggiano's," he said.

Great, a long dinner, kill me now.

At dinner, I sat quietly listening to Linda and my dad go on and on. Linda was the adult version of Becca. She was so unlike my mom, exact opposites. I was like my mom. Why did the attractive blondes always get the guys? Even if I dyed my hair blonde, I still wouldn't land the guys. I didn't have that goddess look—long and thick wavy hair, big bosom, curvy hips, and long legs. I was trim from all my running and had muscular calves and thighs, but I got short changed in the boob department. My hair was dark brown, long enough for a pony tail, but nothing remarkable. Why was I analyzing all of this? What did it matter? After the salad, I began messing with the napkin in my lap…anything to detach from the situation.

"Are you dating anyone, Brogen?" Ms. Grant asked. Becca sat straight up in her chair, anxious to hear my response.

"Not at this time."

"Well, surely there is a boy who has captured your heart?" she insisted.

I glanced at Becca, and she raised her eyebrow, daring me to say something. "No ma'am."

"Oh, that's a shame. There are some hunky guys at Stanton. Becca has her eyes on this fellow named…"

"Jay, Mother. His name is Jay," Becca replied curtly.

Sigh. I knew it. I waved the surrender flag and threw out any hope of something with Jay.

"She's hoping he'll ask her to the Homecoming Dance."

"I hope you get asked." I meant it. I was done with Jay. She could have him. I liked him, but clearly she was pulling him in like a fish on a hook. Guys like Jay didn't end up with girls like me. My parents were a prime example. My dad married my mom, but he had an affair with the gorgeous blonde. Best to save myself the heartache and forget about Jay. Becca seemed surprised by my response, shocked that I hoped he would ask her.

After that, Becca smiled and tried to make small talk with me. She was relishing in her victory. I was pleasant but in no rush to become friends with her. Hopefully it could just go back to Meg and me conquering our final two years at Stanton, unscathed. The evening ended and they drove me home. I politely said goodbye to Linda, Becca, and my father, and headed into the house. I did not want to do this again. Ever. Maybe tonight's interaction would satisfy my dad for the next five years, so I could crawl back under my little rock of safety.

"Well, how was it?" Mom asked as she rounded the corner.

"Tolerable. He has a new girlfriend, and her daughter goes to my school. He thought we should all meet."

"Hmm, I wonder if they are getting serious."

I could sense her energy change, which probably meant she was feeling jealous. "I don't know, and frankly, I don't care. Like I said before, I don't need him in my life. I don't want him in my life." I didn't need to worry for Mom. She was an adult, and she was cute and smart. She could get a guy if she put some effort into it. I had my own pity party to host.

"You okay?" she asked.

I looked at Mom and smiled the best I could. "Yeah, I am. Awkward night. I think I'll go soak in the tub."

"Okay, love you, sweetie." I returned her affection with a kiss on the cheek.

In the tub, I let the hot, soapy suds wrap me in a warm hug. I felt the weight of the evening seep away with the bubbles, and I began to think a bit clearer. I wondered how school would be on Monday since Becca and I shared a moment at dinner. Would she actually talk to me? Would we act as if we were complete strangers? And what about Jay? Could I watch her making moves on him and see him falling for her? Could I let him go?

The image of my mom's jealous face tonight was proof enough I should protect myself from the heartache and stay away from guys like Jay. I stayed in the tub a few minutes more and realized tonight was a blessing. I got to see what my future would be like if I made the mistake of falling for Jay. I put on my pjs, played some music, and grabbed my sketchbook for my nightly sketch.

Chapter 6

The week flew by and Friday arrived before I knew it. The week was full of usual high school busyness, with the added excitement of the upcoming Homecoming Dance. Becca wore shorter skirts, higher heels, tighter shirts, and touched Jay every chance she had. She would surely win him over before the dance next week. Maybe they would even be the Homecoming King and Queen. Wouldn't that be a riot—the two new kids come in and take over Homecoming Court.

Jay had stopped bumping into me. Although I missed it and the zings I felt inside when he touched me, I was glad we didn't have to experience any weird moments of me pushing him away. It just kind of stopped.

"Come on! Hurry and get your stuff so we can get out of here. Girls' night of pizza, movie, and sleepover is about to start," Meg said as she walked me to my locker.

I was excited to do a girls' night with Meg, and glad my mom was fine with it. "Cool your jets, lady. The movie is not till seven, we have plenty of time." I spun my combination lock and opened the creaky metal door. Then, like a leaf falling from a tree, a blue scrap of paper floated down from the top vent slot. Meg grabbed it before I could.

We need to talk.
- J

I felt the color drain from my face. I'd avoided him most of the week. I hated confrontation. Why couldn't he go be with Becca and leave it alone?

"What's this about?" Meg asked.

"No clue. Listen, if you want girls' night to happen fast, though, you need to speed me past Jay as if our houses were on fire. Otherwise, I'll be chatting all night, and girls' night will be ruined." I was fibbing, but I knew Meg would do whatever was needed to save girls' night, and I couldn't talk to Jay.

We left through the front doors, and I saw Jay leaning against a nearby tree, chatting with one of the swim team guys. Jay's circle of friends was growing exponentially with ties to track, thanks to Soren, and now the swim team. His teammate spied us coming out the door and pointed in our direction. Jay turned and a smile quickly crossed his lips. He pushed away from the tree and approached us.

"Brogen. Meg." He nodded at both of us, and Meg paused on the steps. I gave her arm a tug to remind her we did not want to stop girls' night for anything, but Meg was like a deer trapped in headlights. "Brogen, can I talk to you for a moment?"

"Sorry, we have big plans tonight and are already late."

He let his head fall in disappointment, then quickly recovered and tried again. "I can keep it short. Please, just two minutes."

"Brogen, two minutes shouldn't make us late," Meg said. I pinched her. "Ow! What was that for?"

"Traitor," I muttered to Meg. Then I turned back to Jay. "Two minutes. That's it." I stormed off to find a quiet spot away from nosey ears. Jay followed and caught up. When we got out of hearing range I spun to face him. "What do you want?" I realized I didn't sound like my usual self, but I really didn't want to have this conversation.

"Did I do something to piss you off?" he asked. That was it? He stared at me, waiting for an answer.

"No. You have not done anything to piss me off."

"Are you bipolar?"

"What?" I yelled. Some heads turned, and I quickly brought my voice down. "No, why the hell would you think that?"

"Because I like you. I mean, I liked you. I liked the Brogen I met at the rabid dog party." I couldn't help chuckle at the fact he called it a party. I still hadn't found the right word to term that strange night. "After that, I felt like I was really getting to know you, and I liked you. Smart, beautiful, not caught up in the high school drama, funny." I looked up at him and felt my heart flutter. No one had ever said things like this to me. "Then one day, you start ignoring me, like you have no desire to even care I exist. I don't get it."

I couldn't look into his hazel eyes anymore—too much emotion and energy coming off him. "I had no idea you felt that way." I was trying to think of what to say next. His statement gave me hope that maybe we had a chance together.

"Listen, the Homecoming Dance is next Saturday. I'm gonna go with my swim buddies and just have a night out. Take this week to think about what you want. If you show up to the dance, I'll take it as a green light to go forward with our relationship. If you don't, I'll accept that you have no interest in knowing me, and I'll leave you be."

"I thought you'd be going with Becca. I mean, she really likes you."

"She does?" Jay's face contorted into a forced look of shock. We both bust out laughing. "I'm sure Becca wants me to take her, but there's nothing between us." He looked at me sincerely. "Think about it, and I hope to see you Saturday." He winked and then walked away.

Meg raced over to me. "What did he want?"

I was melting inside, from being close to him, from his words, from his proposition. "I'll tell you on the walk home."

That night we stayed up late talking about what I should do with my Jay situation.

"I say yes, go to the dance. I'll go with you. Jay is a good guy. I mean, he even took the attack of a rabid dog for you. All good in my book," Meg said.

"But what if I end up like my mom? I think her heart hurts far worse since she truly loved my dad, and he turned around and cheated on her with

Blondezilla. I don't think I could handle that."

"Well, good thing this is high school and not marriage. You can make stupid mistakes without super long-lasting effects."

"True. I'm probably making a bigger deal about it."

"I think the boys swim team has a home meet on Wednesday. Let's go see him and cheer him on. Drop a hint that he has won your heart," Meg suggested. I threw one of her stuffed animals at her, which went into a full-blown pillow/stuffed animal fight.

That night I dreamt of Jay, sitting on the curb with blood dripping out of each of his bite marks, smiling at me as if he had not a care in the world. It was haunting to see him so marred, so bloody. Yet his face was calm and uplifting. I wish I understood dream symbolism, because I'm sure there were all kinds of meanings to uncover. I brushed it off as my subconscious burning off my anxieties.

***

On Wednesday, Meg and I went to the Aquatic Center where the swim meet was in full swing. The crowd on Stanton's side was plentiful. The visiting team had mostly parents from their team cheering. We found seats in the second row. The best seats were up high, because they had a better view of the entire pool, but they were all occupied. Jay was competing in three events—the freestyle relay, the one hundred-meter breaststroke, and the fifty-meter freestyle. The fifty-meter freestyle was like a sprint, and it was the first event he was competing in. Jay walked past us on the way to the starting block, and Meg hollered his name. He turned and locked eyes with me. The smile that grew on his face was beautiful. I was in trouble. How could I resist this guy? He looked amazing in his team suit, trim with broad shoulders.

He took his spot on the block, shook his limbs loose, and dove in at the starting tone. He swam like a fish. He swam so fast and only took a single breath. His speed and lung capacity helped him win the heat. Meg and I jumped up clapping. His teammates congratulated him. He took off his goggles and went to talk to his coach. His coach patted his back and continued chatting a bit longer, then the team medic came over and studied Jay's face. Jay glanced over at us and had a grim look on his face. From our seats, nothing looked visibly wrong. There was head shaking, arguing, and in the end, Jay lost the argument. He threw his goggles down and stormed off.

"What the hell's going on? Did he disqualify?" Meg asked.

"I don't know. I don't think so. Why would they need the medic for a disqualification?"

We gathered our stuff and ran out of the meet to see if we could find Jay. We looked everywhere, but we couldn't find him. I went back to the pool area and pulled one of his teammates aside to ask what happened. They didn't know any details but heard he was pulled from the meet for an injury.

"I don't get it. He looked good and even won the event. Jay looked mad at their decision and walked out of there on his own. Must not be too bad," I said.

"I wonder why they were looking at his face. Maybe he got cut on something," Meg commented. I nodded. It was probably something simple like that and they didn't want blood in the pool. I could ask him the next day at school.

Thursday morning, I was anxious to see if Jay was okay. I passed by his locker and saw his teammates surrounding him and laughing. Jay looked up and had a pair of sunglasses on.

"C'mon, Wilken, let's see it," one of his teammates said. Jay took off the sunglasses and had blood in his eyes and bruising on his cheeks.

"Jesus, you look like you got in a fight and ate a knuckle sandwich," his buddy remarked. I stood frozen and staring.

"Brogen!" He shoved his sunglasses back on.

"What happened?" I stammered out. I was horrified. He looked awful, and it scared me.

"I'm okay. They call it a subjuncta something or other. Basically, I popped a blood vessel in my eye and my face. Guess I pushed myself too hard to impress a girl."

I lifted the glasses from his face and gently traced my fingers along his bruised cheek. "You look awful. Put these back on. What's the treatment?"

He put the shades back on. "It should go away in a week. You wait it out like any bruise. I'll look awesomely scary for the dance Saturday. Too bad it's not a Halloween dance."

I laughed at his joke. He always saw the bright

side of things. "That was an impressive swim. Are you allowed to swim again, or is there a chance this can happen again?"

"Oh, I'm gonna swim again, but maybe not as hard as I did at the meet. So, if you don't mind, hold that awesome spectacle in your mind forever when you think of me swimming." Jay looked awful, but he was always a bright ray of sunshine, and I felt better just being in his presence.

"Sure," I replied. I saw Becca approaching and decided to take that moment to break away. "See ya around, Nemo." Jay smiled as I walked away, and Becca glared at me. I chose to look away quickly and head to my locker.

When I saw Meg later in the day, I told her about Jay's injury.

"No wonder he was wearing sunglasses. That's nuts. Guess he was trying to make a good impression on you. Are you still up for hitting the mall tomorrow night to find a dress for the dance?"

"Yeah, sounds good. I hope it's not weird on Saturday. Becca gave me a poisonous glare when I was talking to Jay earlier."

"Ahh, don't worry about her. I'll be there. Besides, she doesn't have him yet, so technically, you're not stealing him away," Meg pointed out.

"True. I'm not trying to steal him from anyone. There's just this thing between us. I can't explain it."

"There's definitely something between the two of you. You'd have to be an idiot not to see it. Anyway, I'll pick you up around six thirty."

***

Friday night arrived, and Mom was so excited I was going to a school dance she gave me $150 toward an outfit. Meg picked me up at 6:30 p.m. sharp. "I should not go and just keep the cash. I can't believe she gave me that much for a single outfit."

"Where's the fun in that? Plus, you got a guy waiting on you Saturday, can't disappoint him," Meg teased.

We were approaching the area of town where the mall was when Meg's phone rang. She fumbled in her purse while driving.

"Eyes on the road, lady. I'll find it," I chided. Digging past her birth control and gum, I saw the blinking phone. Then I heard Meg scream.

Chapter 7

My head felt like it had exploded and been glued back together. My chest hurt with every breath. My arm felt cold from the frigid IV fluid running into my veins. There were bandages on both of my arms, and the smell of antiseptic burned my nose. I was in the hospital and in rotten shape. But where was everyone? Where was my mom? Where was Meg? I pushed the call button on my remote. After what felt like fifteen million minutes, a nurse came in with my mom.

"Oh thank God, you're awake. How do you feel, sweetie?" my mom asked with concern and love-filled eyes.

"I've been better. What the hell happened?"

My mom looked to the nurse and gave a little nod.

"I'll fetch the doctor," the nurse said and turned away.

"Mom. What's going on? Where's Meg? How did I get here?"

"Oh, sweetie. You and Meg were in a terrible car

accident." She stopped talking to hold back her emotion, but her tears fell anyway. "I can't believe I almost lost you. I love you so much."

"I love you too. Is Meg okay?"

She grabbed my hand and held it. "She is in worse shape than you. The impact was on her side of the car. She's in a coma in the ICU."

Now the tears fell down my face. I had no words. Meg was like my sister. I felt sick to my stomach with grief. I let go of Mom's hand and covered my face to hide my sorrow. Mom rubbed my back in comfort. After I was able to compose myself, I asked, "Can I see her?"

"Well, we'll have to ask the doctor when he comes in. I've been up to see her a few times. Her parents have not left her side since she was brought in. I asked them to text me if there were any changes in her condition, which reminds me...I need to let them know you are awake." Mom took out her phone and began texting. A doctor walked in at that moment and introduced himself.

"Hello, I'm Dr. Black. I'm here to check on you. Is now a good time?" I nodded, but felt like my head might pop as I shook it. "How is your pain on a scale of one to ten, ten being the worst pain you could ever imagine?"

"Well, when I nod my head, the head pain is at a seven—not nodding it's at a three."

"And what about the rest of your body?"

"Well, my arms are a two, but when I move them it feels tight, like the skin is pulling, and becomes a five. My ribs are a four, but a seven when I take a deep breath."

He made notes of each number on my chart, and then approached to check my pupils. "The pupils are responding better, so she is definitely on the mend. I need to ask you some questions." I nodded slightly, enough to acknowledge him but not cause level seven pain. "What's your name?"

"Brogen."

"How old are you?"

"Seventeen."

"Where do you go to school?"

"I'm a junior at Stanton High."

"What do you last remember before waking up in the hospital?"

I sighed and searched my brain for the answer to that question. My brain felt muddled. "There was a phone call. Wait. First, Meg and I were headed to the mall to get dresses for the dance. Then her phone rang. The dance…" I trailed off the end of my sentence, lost in the thought of Jay waiting for me to show up. "She searched for her phone, and I told her to watch the road while I look for it." Tears began falling down my face. Stupid phone.

Mom rushed over, sat next to me on the bed, and grabbed my hand. "Brogen, Meg was broadsided by a drunk driver. Witnesses said the drunk ran a red light and hit you guys at about fifty miles an hour. I'm not sure Meg could have avoided the accident." My eyes grew big and I stared at her.

The doctor remarked, "You were lucky you both were wearing your seatbelts. You hit the side window with your head and sustained a simple skull fracture, a bruised rib, and needed stitches in both your upper arms from glass cuts. It could have been so much worse for you had it not been for the airbag and seatbelt."

"And Meg? Do you know what happened with her? What her injuries are?" I asked.

"She is still unconscious. Her head injury was a little more severe. Besides that, I cannot share any details."

"When can I see her?"

"Probably not until you are released. If you continue to heal as well as you have, you'll probably say goodbye to me on Thursday," he said.

"Thursday? What's today?"

"Monday," Mom said. "You've been unconscious for three days."

I was shocked that I missed three days of my life. "What happened to the drunk driver?"

"He died in the accident." It was cruel to be relieved, but his death meant that no others would be at risk due to his poor choice to drink and drive.

"Let's let her rest," the doctor advised.

"Will you be all right while I run home for a shower and change of clothes?" Mom asked.

"Yeah, Mom, I'll be fine. Can you bring my pillow from home?"

"You bet. I love you, baby." Mom leaned over to kiss my forehead.

***

The next few days passed quickly. It was a nice vacation from school, and I got to watch trashy talk shows in the hospital bed and be a lazy loaf while my body healed. I still hurt when I moved, and I was not the prettiest thing to look at; my bruises were yellowing and I needed a proper shower. When Thursday finally arrived, I got the 'all clear' to head home. Mom wheeled me in a wheelchair to the ICU to visit Meg. Her parents were sitting in chairs reading—her dad read a magazine, and her mom read a book out loud to Meg.

"Hello Mr. and Mrs. Taylor," I said. They both turned and got up to give me gentle hugs.

"We were so glad to hear you had improved and now get to go home," Mrs. Taylor remarked.

"How is Meg?" She looked like she went a few rounds with Rocky Balboa and was sleeping it off.

"She's improving. She has finally started to keep her oxygen levels up and is swallowing her saliva. They removed the intubation tube yesterday. That means she is becoming more conscious. We are hopeful she'll progress more rapidly since the swelling is decreasing."

"The doctor wouldn't share her injuries with me. What's wrong?" I asked.

"Meg had bleeding on the brain. They operated to relieve the pressure. She also lost some skin and had to have a skin graft on her thighs. I can't believe you both were in that terrible accident." Meg's mom teared up.

I squeezed her hand for support. "Would it be all right if I visited Meg after school each day for a few hours?"

"Actually, that would be great, but only if you are up for it."

I reached my hand to Meg's foot and wiggled her socked big toe. "See you guys soon. Love you,

Meg." They said goodbye and Mom wheeled me to the car.

As we drove home, I watched the leaves fall to the ground, littering the front lawns with their colorful debris. It was hard to believe I had missed almost a week of life on the outside. The air was damp and cool with the fall weather in full force— sweater weather. We turned down the street where Jay's aunt and uncle lived. I looked at their house as we drove past, but Jay and Soren were at school, and his aunt and uncle were probably at work. I remembered Jay asking me to come to the dance to prove I wanted to move forward with our relationship. I not only failed to make the dance, I was MIA for the whole next week. What would he think? Becca had probably made her move on him that night and my chance was blown. Oh well. Right now, I needed to figure out how to get back into the swing of things and how to help Meg. I took it easy the rest of the weekend and worked on the homework Mom picked up from the school earlier in the week. It was slow going, and I needed lots of rest and breaks.

On Monday, I woke up a little earlier so I didn't have to rush around everywhere. I was going to get my stitches out after school when I went to visit Meg, and I didn't want to mess them up before then. At school, I went to the office to turn in my doctor's note admitting me back to school and dismissing me from gym for two weeks.

"You are fortunate to have survived that crash. They had a write up in the paper this morning about your accident and the dangers of drunk driving."

The office secretary showed me the newspaper article. The car was crumpled like it was made out of aluminum. To the right of the article there was a photo of the deceased drunk driver. I nearly choked. It was the same drunk who hit the rabid dog. I had so many emotions flying through me. I was relieved he was dead. I was angry at the cops for letting him off lightly when he hit the dog. I was mad at myself for being grateful his drunk ass came along when it did and hit that dog. And now the idiot drank too much, plowed into us, nearly killed us, and killed himself.

"Thank you for showing me this. This is the first time I have seen the accident. It looks awful."

"Oh, sweetie. You must have been so traumatized. How's your friend?"

"She's still trying to pull through. I'm going to visit her after school today."

She smiled. "Well, good luck today, and if you need anything, just ask."

I smiled back at her and exited out the office door. The bell for first period rang, and I was grateful for the quiet chance to go to my locker before class. As I rounded the corner, I saw a tall, slender guy leaning against my locker. It was Jay.

Chapter 8

"Are you skipping class?" I asked.

He turned around and his jaw fell open. Jay's face twisted with disbelief and…wonder. He quickly took two steps toward me, grabbed my face, and pressed his lips against mine. It was such an innocent kiss but there was so much love felt in that intimate moment.

"I saw the paper this morning. You didn't show for the dance, and I was angry that I read your signals wrong. I thought for sure you'd be there, but you never showed. Then you were out the whole week. I didn't know what happened to you. Becca spread some B.S. rumors about you moving in with your dad and wanting to switch schools because you didn't like the kids here. I thought she was crazy, but as the week went on, it was easier to believe. I never should have believed her."

This was the most I'd ever heard come out of his mouth. Ever.

"Are you okay?" he asked.

I nodded.

"This last week sucked. First I thought you wanted nothing to do with me, then Becca tells me you moved away, and then I find out you were in some horrid accident. No moving away, and no more accidents." He looked so intensely at me, I found it hard to breathe.

"I'll try my best. Did you see that the guy who hit us was the same one who hit the dog?"

"Son of a…" Jay punched the locker next to me. "They went too easy on that jerk. *We* went too easy on him. Makes me sick to my stomach. I'm so glad you are okay." Jay glanced at the photo and let out a rush of air. "This crash looks so bad, like no one could have survived."

I sighed and looked down. "Meg is still fighting to come back. She's still unconscious. It's hard to be back here when I just want to be at the hospital holding her hand."

Jay wrapped me in a hug. "You can visit her though, right?"

"Yeah, I plan to go after school. I get my stitches out today, so I'll pop in to see her then. Hey, speaking of injuries, your eyes look much better."

Jay smirked. "Yeah, no more creepy blood eyes. My aunt took me to the doc, and he said it would clear up on its own. And…it did. 'Thanks doc, here's a thousand bucks for nothin'.'"

"At least it wasn't anything permanent or dangerous. But you should quit trying so hard to impress the ladies, you might end up in the hospital."

Jay chuckled. "The doc took some blood while I was there to make sure I don't have any weird deficiencies or mutations. I wonder if he can detect someone trying too hard to impress a girl in those blood samples," Jay said, beaming down at me with his big eyes.

"Excuse me, you two need to get to class...*now*," the sophomore language arts teacher reprimanded.

"Sorry, ma'am," Jay said to the teacher. Then he turned to me. "Let's get to class." Luckily we had first period together—it bought us two more minutes of talk time. We agreed to eat lunch outside together at one of the picnic tables. Jay wanted to hear more about the accident, and lunch granted us twenty minutes to tell the tale.

I showed up late to lunch because my teacher asked about the accident. When I walked into the cafeteria, I saw Jay and Soren sitting with Becca and the Blonde-squad. Maybe the lunch talk wasn't going to happen. Funny how the drama of high school seemed to always exist. I kind of missed my carefree week in the hospital, watching trashy talk shows. I went through the lunch line, picked up a PB&J and some fruit, and then sat at the table Meg and I ate at. Some of the kids at the table were talking to me about how I was feeling and asking about Meg. I didn't mind telling them, they were a lot like Meg and me—independent, smart, and creative, but socially awkward. As I was telling them about waking up in the hospital, I noticed all eyes left me and were looking at a point above my head. I stopped mid-sentence and looked up to see Jay standing behind me. He seemed disappointed.

"I thought we had lunch plans," he said.

"So did I," I returned flatly.

"Did you change your mind or something?" He sounded irritated.

"No, I saw you sitting with your friends and assumed you had changed your mind."

"You weren't here yet. So I sat down and was telling Soren and the others that I had other lunch plans. That's it."

I felt like an idiot. Way to make a big deal out of nothing. "Sorry, I guess I jumped to conclusions." I turned to the lunch table. "Sorry guys, I'll finish this story tomorrow. See ya."

Jay carried my tray and we went outside to a picnic table. It was rather crisp outside, so Jay sat next to me, allowing our body heat to radiate off each other's. The cool air scared off the other students, and we had the patio area to ourselves.

"So tell me what happened to you guys."

"Well, I had every intention of going to the dance." A smile grew across his face. "Meg was going to join me, so we were off to look for dresses. I remember her phone rang, and she started to dig for it…I told her to drive while I searched for it, and that's all I remember of that night."

"What happened next?" he asked, intrigued.

"I woke up in the hospital with my brain pounding and painful ribs. They said I had a simple skull fracture from hitting the side window, stitches in both arms from the glass, and bruised ribs."

"So no PE for a while?"

"I get two weeks off so my head can fully heal."

"Put some scar ointment on those wounds once you get those stitches out. I've had a heck of a time healing from mine." Jay rolled up his sleeves, and I saw white and pink paper-thin scars up and down his arms in the pattern of a dog jaw. "I keep putting vitamin E on them, but I think I'll just have to remember our rabid dog party forever."

"Oh, that still looks terrible. So sorry. They must have been deep bites." I noticed Jay's skin looked very thin all over. His veins looked like a road map up his arm.

"I don't think so. The doc said my skin tore really easily, and it was hard to get the stitches to take…said it was like I didn't have any glue holding me together. I think it's something funky my body does. Maybe they'll figure it out with the blood they drew when my bloody eyes happened."

"I don't know, sounds like nothing to worry about. So you need to not swim so hard, or you get bloody eyes, and your skin tears, so no more rabid dog parties. At least it's not cancer. I mean, you look healthy."

"Yeah, I think they are making a big deal out of nothing too." Jay bumped against me gently. "Lunch is almost over, let's get rid of our trays."

"Hey, wait. I think it's only fair that you to tell me how you came to Stanton. Tomorrow? Lunch?" I smiled.

Jay looked at me hesitantly and then agreed. "Okay, and tomorrow—no misunderstandings."

Chapter 9

After school, Mom took me to the hospital to get my stitches removed, and we stopped by the ICU to check on Meg. The stitches were no picnic to get out, but the doctor who stitched me up did a great job. I already healed better than Jay. He could keep his vitamin E since I didn't seem to need it. Meg was in the same position but wore different socks today. Meg's mom was reading a book in the chair by the window.

"Hey, Mrs. Taylor." Meg's mom rose and hugged my mom and me. "Any changes?"

"Actually, she squeezed my hand earlier when I told her I loved her." Mrs. Taylor got teary eyed. "They say that's a great sign."

"Oh, I'm so glad to hear this," I said. I needed Meg to pull through.

"I'm here to take you for a break and get some coffee while Brogen spends some time with Meg," Mom said to Mrs. Taylor. Mrs. Taylor nodded, then stood and grabbed her purse.

"So, Meg, I'm not gonna lie, you look terrible.

But a little makeup and a proper shower would take you back to the first class dame you were before the accident. Anyway, today was my first day back at school. Same drama, different day. Ooh, there is something new...Jay kissed me. Just an innocent kiss. I think he was glad to see me alive. I'm trying not to overthink it." I paused and moved closer to her side. "They had a picture in the paper of the wreck, and it looked bad. Anyway, you need to get better. School sucks without you, and I miss you. You can do it, Meg, keep fighting."

I snuggled up near the foot of the bed, careful not to move or touch her, grabbed a Glamour magazine, and read her some of the articles and quizzes. Mom and Mrs. Taylor came back, and Mrs. Taylor appeared more relaxed. Mom and her amazing psychologist skills had a way of calming people. Mom gave me a little wink.

"I'm so grateful you girls came to visit. Do come again." I hugged Mrs. Taylor and kissed Meg on the head.

As we walked to the car Mom said, "You're a pretty awesome kid. Glad you're mine."

"That's pretty funny, Mom, because I was thinking the same thing...I am pretty awesome." We both laughed. "Actually, I thought the same about you. You are very good for people." She gave me a side hug. "Do you think Meg's gonna be okay?"

"I believe so. She's definitely headed in the right direction. Let's go home for some dinner."

Dinner consisted of grilled chicken breast, rolls, and a tossed salad. We laughed and joked about odd things that happened in my younger years. I felt so much lighter than I had prior to the accident. Energies and emotions of others weren't getting in like they used to. I actually felt "normal." After helping with the dishes, I watched a sitcom with my mom before heading to my room.

That night I lay awake. When I closed my eyes, I saw Jay at my locker and the intense look in his eyes. His sudden kiss. There was a connection between us. Tomorrow I'd hear more about his past and get more pieces of his puzzle. Hopefully his parents weren't serial killers who were locked up for a killing spree, and he was sent away to learn the trade from his aunt and uncle. I liked Jay and I didn't want that to change. But what brought him to Stanton? Questions and thoughts swirled around in my head, and I finally fell asleep adrift in the sea of unknown.

First period algebra was exciting—not the algebra part, but the Jay part. I kept checking my peripheral vision and saw him looking my way. Twice I looked up and caught him staring at me, dead on. But instead of trying to hide it, he smiled. It made me laugh because most guys would try to be more subtle, but Jay seemed happy to get caught. What was his deal? Becca was in the next row over, glaring at us, but I couldn't care less. I had survived a car crash and was not going to let her get in my head.

I was actually on time for lunch and searched around for Jay but didn't see him. I went through the lunch line and grabbed a hotdog and chips. While heading to my table, I peeked out the window and saw Jay sitting at the picnic table we occupied yesterday. Soren was talking with him. I went out and greeted them.

"Anyway, see ya after school, Jay. Later, Brogen." Soren grabbed his tray and left the table.

"See ya, Soren." I sat down across from Jay. Today was warmer, so I didn't need his body heat to warm me. "So...I'm all ears. What chain of events has led you to the lovely Stanton High?"

Jay smiled at me. "Sure you wanna hear this? You might cry."

He's teasing. Why would I cry?

"Yeah, I'm curious...and I'm a big girl."

"Well, I grew up in a happy home in a town not too far from here. My parents both worked and made good money. I never wanted for anything. We lived in a nice house with a huge backyard."

"Sounds pretty good so far," I interrupted.

"I always had an easy time making friends, so I always had a playmate around when I was young. Mom was a lawyer, and Dad was a drug sales rep." So far everything sounded great. He paused and pushed around his food and took a sip of his Coke. I stared at him and read his energy. He was really struggling with this next part. I reached out my hand and held his hand in mine to let him know I was there to support him. "My mom died suddenly three years ago from an aneurysm. She was only thirty-nine years old. My dad did his best to be a single parent while grieving his wife. I'm not sure he grieved enough. A year later, he would come home and lose himself in a bottle of Jack. I tried helping him, but it usually ended badly and I would just

65

make sure he ended up in his bed to sleep it off."

"Oh my God, I am so sorry." I would have never imagined Jay's mom died.

"So last summer, he must've stopped off at a bar on his way home from work. He was plastered, and I was so pissed that he drove drunk. I dumped his booze down the drain, and he punched me in the face. Split my cheek open. The next day, when my dad was sober, he saw what he'd done to me. He promised me he would be a better dad and was going to go into rehab. So Soren's parents offered to let me live with them till my dad got clean." Jay looked at me and must have seen the tear forming in my eye. "I told you, you might cry."

I snickered and nodded. "Boy, I don't get it. I mean, you've been through more than most kids our age, and yet there is this radiant, positive energy coming from you. People are drawn to you. You're so charismatic. You don't let that awful stuff taint you. How do you do it?"

"And there goes my hat size. Thank you for inflating my head." He laughed. "Thanks for the compliment, but this is who I am. I don't know how to be any different."

"Well, I am truly sorry you've had to go through all of that. Sounds like your dad's turning things around, and hopefully he will appreciate the son he has and be there for him. Your mom died really young. Does your family have heart problems, or was hers random?"

"Her death was a shock to the family. No one had died young like her. We all tend to live into our eighties."

"It must have been hard to lose your mom."

"It was, it is. I miss her all the time." Jay sat up a little straighter, and I could feel his energy change. "Anyway, that's my story. It's not a secret, but please don't broadcast it to everyone."

"No worries, thanks for sharing it with me. I feel like I got a huge piece of the Jay puzzle handed to me."

"Jay puzzle, huh? Not much to figure out here," he laughed.

"I beg to differ." The bell rang. "Time to finish this day. Thanks for confiding in me," I said.

Jay and I walked inside to dump our trays. I made a pit stop in the restroom before heading to my locker. That was a heavy piece of info Jay dropped on me. As I washed my hands, the bathroom door opened and in walked Becca and two of her Blonde-squad friends.

"Ahh, Brogen, I've been wanting to have a little chat with you," Becca said in her sing-song voice.

"Oh yeah? Are you disappointed I didn't move out of state or whatever the heck that rumor was you were spreading?" I snapped.

"Ooh, snippy, snippy. Did the accident knock something loose in that head of yours? I'm wanting to talk about you and Jay. Was I wrong to read your hints that Jay and I had the green light to get together? Because this little lunch date you two have shared...doesn't fly with me."

"You don't own him. Apparently you're too shallow for him to be interested in. You've flung your hair, boosted your boobs, shaken your butt, and he *still* seems to gravitate toward me. Guess Jay cares a little more about what's inside than some stupid, superficial Blondezilla."

I stormed past her, slamming the restroom door behind me. Somewhere in the middle of my next class, I ran through the bathroom interaction in my head. I would have never been able to stand up to someone like Becca at the beginning of the year. I was much more empowered. Maybe the accident had changed something inside of me. I wasn't going to hide or cower in the corner anymore.

***

The day dragged on, and I was finally able to visit Meg. To my surprise, she was awake.

"Did I just miss Prince Charming? True love's kiss to awaken you?" I teased. Meg smiled so genuinely at me that I warmed head to toe. I squeezed her hand and rubbed her head. "Seriously, when did you wake up?"

"A couple of hours ago. I feel like barf, though."

I laughed. Her mom excused herself so we could catch up. I took in the room, which had the same monitors I had, a few cards, and twenty new stuffed animals for Meg to add to her hoarding collection. I couldn't help but chuckle to myself. Whoever married Meg had better allow at least half of her stuffed animals in the house or they'd never make it. "Well, you'll get better. You really had me scared."

"I'm so sorry I got us in that accident. Are you okay?" Meg asked.

I couldn't believe Meg was apologizing. "Hold

up—that accident was in *no* way your fault. We were broadsided by a drunk driver. Actually, it was the same drunk who hit the dog that attacked Jay and me. He didn't survive the crash."

"No shit. We could have died. Why didn't they lock that guy away?" Meg was getting upset.

"I know, they went light on him when he hit the dog. Maybe they will reevaluate how they punish drunk drivers after knowing what happened to us," I added. "Let's not think about that right now. You need to stay calm and heal enough to get out of this joint."

Meg studied me. "Are you all the way okay? I'll feel sick if there's permanent damage."

I laughed. "Well, the answer to that question depends on who you ask. Meg, I'm good. I am almost done with my two week break from PE, and I plan to start running again this weekend. My stitches are out and I've healed nicely. And I grew a pair…stood up to Becca today in the restroom at school."

"Spill it. I've been down for the count for a few weeks and am desperate to play catch up on my favorite lifetime drama." I giggled and then recounted the events that occurred between Jay, Becca, and myself. "Okay, I'm so going to kick butt and get out of here. I need to see this drama with my own eyes. So are you and Jay an item now? I mean, you kissed…"

"I'm pretty sure that kiss was not an 'I wanna love you forever and make you my wife' kiss. It was a 'Phew! I thought you were dead' kiss."

Meg laughed. "Like I said, I gotta see it with my

own eyes. You seem different, way better. Maybe you should be thanking me for risking your life and helping you 'grow a pair.'"

"I'm glad we are both okay. So, when are they going to do the graft?"

"It's done. When I began improving they decided to do it while I was still unconscious. I think I'm stuck here for the rest of the week if it continues to heal well."

"Well, I promise I will visit and keep you informed of the high school drama unfolding at Stanton."

"You better. Love you, Brogen." I squeezed her hand.

Meg's mom returned. "Did I come back too early?"

"No, I need to head home and work on homework. Good luck tomorrow, Meg. Love you." I bent over and kissed her forehead. "Night, Mrs. Taylor."

I drove home from the hospital and wanted to spend time with my mom. Thankfully, she didn't have any patients tonight. When I got home, I opened the door to the house and the delicious smells of dinner filled my nose.

"Either I am beyond hungry, or you made a world class meal tonight. Either way, I can't wait to eat." Mom gave me a smile and plated the food. "Need any help?"

"Grab our drinks and bring them to the table, please. I'm sure you're hungry, but I'm hoping it's worthy of world class status too." Mom set down the plates of sautéed garlic asparagus, homemade double mashed potatoes, and grilled steak. "How was your day? You look good, so it must have been positive."

I shoved a piece of steak in my mouth, chewed, and nodded. She was going to have to wait as I enjoyed this delicious bite. Once I had it down, I answered, "Meg's awake."

"Oh, that's wonderful. When can she come home?"

Now Mom had to wait while I enjoyed a bite of asparagus. This made her laugh. Maybe I really was super hungry. "She had her skin graft, so she should be out within the week if she keeps healing well."

"Ugh, I forgot about the skin graft. Poor kid."

"Mom, outstanding job on this food."

Mom chuckled at my remarks and devouring of the food. "Thanks, it does taste pretty good." Mom went in the kitchen for more asparagus. She returned and asked me how the rest of my day went. I hadn't talked about Jay yet, because there hadn't been anything brewing there, but now seemed like a good time to mention him.

"Hey, Mom, remember when I was attacked by that dog a few months ago?" Mom nodded. "Well, the guy that came to my rescue and was attacked— do you remember his name is Jay?"

"Vaguely. What about him?" she probed.

"Well, I guess he saw the pictures of the crash in the paper and thought I had died. When he saw me at school the first day back, he was waiting by my locker."

"Waiting by your locker?" Okay, Mom thought it was strange too.

"And when he saw me, he kissed me." Mom's eyebrows raised. "It wasn't romantic. It was a 'thank God you're alive' kiss." Mom smiled at me like she didn't believe me. "What? I'm telling you, that's the message I got from the kiss."

"Okay, okay, so then what?"

"Well, nothing really. We've talked a little over lunch. But there's this other girl that has her eyes on him. It's Becca. Remember the daughter of Dad's new girlfriend?" Mom rolled her eyes but nodded her head. In that moment, I read Mom's energy—she was worried the story of her and Dad was repeating. "Anyway, she didn't like Jay and me chatting together, so she confronted me in the bathroom."

"And?" Mom was listening intently.

"I was sick of her crap and cowering around her. I let my feelings spill and told her off."

"Wow! That must have been what I sensed in you. You seemed so different sitting at the table tonight, stronger. I'm proud of you." She hesitated. "But, I'm worried about you and this Jay guy. He sounds nice, but are you sure you just don't feel indebted to him for saving you?"

I had not considered that. "I don't know. I know that can happen, and there definitely seems to be a bond between us. Did the bond naturally form, or did the dog party create it? I don't know."

"Dog party?" Mom snickered. "That's what you call it?"

I smiled and nodded. "Rabid dog party, actually."

"Ah. Well, why was this Becca coming after

you? Do she and Jay have a relationship together?" she asked.

"No. Becca and Jay are the new kids, and she has her eyes set on him. That's it."

"Sounds like Jay is fair game, and he needs to pick for himself who he would rather be with. Just keep being yourself, and keep your distance from that Becca girl. Sometimes girls will get nasty if their prize is taken away."

"Agreed. Thanks, Mom." I cleared the table as Mom began scrubbing the dishes. The kitchen phone rang and Mom took a break to answer it. I cleaned off the table and took Mom's spot at the sink. Mom's voice was raising a bit, and she was standing with her back to me.

"Yes, she's fine Philip. Couldn't bother coming by to see her in the hospital, could you?" Mom was talking to my Dad, her ex. "No, she has plans this weekend. I know you want to see her, but it will have to wait another week." She paused, listening to whatever my dad was telling her. "I don't care. Until you start paying child support and making an effort for *her* benefit, I will *not* jump through hoops to get her back in your life. You can play house with your Barbie doll girlfriends, but keep our daughter out of that mess." She slammed the phone down.

I couldn't help it. I started clapping. "Good job, Mom. Looks like you grew a pair too." Mom and I both burst out laughing.

She leaned over and kissed my head. Mom had raised me with some help from my grandma. She worked full-time but managed to attend every school function I ever had. She was all the parent I could ever need. My dad stopped coming to my events when he and my mom divorced. He quit calling me a month later and never took the time to acknowledge my birthday. He was a selfish man distracted by pretty ladies.

"I'm not interested in adding him back in my life. You've been the best mom and dad to me, Mom."

"I love you, baby," she whispered.

Chapter 10

I guess two good days in a row was asking too much. I slept through my alarm and Mom had to drive me to school. When I was walking up the stairs, my sweater snagged on a rough spot on the metal railing, tearing a hole in my sleeve. So irritating. I knew my day would be spent trying to hide the hole and squelching the desire to abandon the sweater even though it was frigid today. Today was a Meg day. I could've used my dear friend to balance me and cheer me up. Soon she would be back to roaming the halls with me.

I walked down the hall and saw Becca and the Blonde-squad snickering nearby. When I turned toward my locker, the word 'SLUT' was written in nail polish on my locker—no doubt placed there by Becca or one of her minions. When I opened the locker, I heard them laughing hysterically. Great. I grabbed my first period folder and walked to the front office without glancing Becca's way.

"Hi, someone wrote something inappropriate on my locker with nail polish. I wondered if the janitor could try and remove it today."

The older desk clerk brought me a half-slip of paper. "Put your name, locker number, and description on here, and then place the form in this basket," she advised me.

"Thanks." I began to fill out the form. I heard the office door open and somebody bumped into me. I looked up to see Jay smiling at me.

"Whatcha doing here, Brogen?" he asked. God he was beautiful. I felt the butterflies in my stomach take flight.

"Maintenance request. Someone decided to do their art project on my locker." Jay's eyebrows went up. Apparently he hadn't been by my locker to see Becca's handy work. "How about you? What's your story?"

"Ah, I have a doctor's appointment this afternoon. Just giving them my slip."

The front office lady came up to take Jay's note. She blushed as she approached him. Did he even know what effect he had on people? "Come down during fifth period and sign out," she told him, avoiding eye contact.

"Thanks." Jay turned to me. "Wanna walk me to my locker?"

"Sure. Hey, I saw Meg yesterday, and she's out of the coma."

"You must be so relieved. When does she come back to school?"

"We think she might come back next week," I told him.

"Hmm, one more week to find out all about Brogen Mathers during lunch...not sure that's enough time."

I rolled my eyes. There was not much to know about me, and he'd be disappointed when he found that out. He walked close enough to me that our upper arms occasionally brushed against each other. "Oh, you planning on eating with me again? What about poor Soren?" I teased.

"Soren's a big boy and has enough friends to never be lonely. And yes, I plan on eating with you again. But…not today. My appointment is around lunch, so I'll miss the whole last half of the day." I was disappointed hearing this. It was nice having someone to talk to at lunch, and I looked forward to the easy banter Jay and I had. Seeing the disappointment in my face, he turned to me and added, "But the next day, I'm all yours. I'll even let you ask me whatever you want. Maybe even my deepest, darkest secret."

"What, that you like to wear girls' panties?" I teased.

Jay laughed but stopped suddenly. His jaw dropped as he stared past me. "What the…"

I followed his eyes and saw him staring at my locker. "I'm guessing Becca. We mixed words in the bathroom yesterday, and I think I pissed her off."

He laughed. "You're such a scrapper. Good for you." He scratched at the letters." What is that? Nail polish?" I shrugged. Jay got his first period books from his locker and we walked to algebra.

"There's the lovey-dovey couple now," our teacher greeted us as we entered class. I felt my face blush far worse than when I read my lovely 'SLUT' message from Becca. The kids in the class did catcalls, and Jay fist bumped a few of his guy friends as he let the comment roll off him untouched. I stared at the floor as I found my way to my desk. Why did it feel like we were a couple now? During algebra I glanced over at Jay a few times, and he'd always look up and smile, like he sensed me looking his way. I decided to be brave and not turn away. I was drinking him in because I wouldn't see him later in the day. I paid no attention to Becca, but she probably tried to kill me with evil glares all period.

After class, Jay waited for me outside of the classroom. "Hey, good luck with the artwork." He gave me a side hug. I was enjoying being around Jay and knew the rest of the day would suck without him.

"Good luck with your doc appointment. Is it a follow up?"

"No, it's for my test results and said they do it by appointment only." He shrugged.

Then, something changed inside of me, like someone had flipped a switch. I felt my heart sink. I felt like vomiting. I felt like if I turned on the news, there would be a report about a nation being wiped out by a nuclear bomb. I had never felt like this in my life. Death, destruction, devastation, all around me. A wave of sorrow washed over me, drowning me.

"Brogen, you okay?" Jay asked.

I nodded, but I wasn't. Truthfully, I didn't know what the hell had happened. It made no sense. Maybe my defenses were down and I was picking up someone's bad energy. Maybe something was wrong with my mom, or Meg. Maybe Jay was going to get in a car accident. I didn't know what to say. I felt like I was going crazy. There was so much negative emotion in me, but anything I might say would sound crazy.

I finally replied with, "Just be careful." I gave him a hug, strong and full of emotion.

He was puzzled but chuckled at my mercurial mood change. "I will. See you tomorrow, babe."

Normally I'd melt from him calling me "babe," but my mind was racing, trying to figure out why I was experiencing this feeling. Jay was off to his next class, and I kicked myself for not getting his phone number. How would I check if he was all right? I couldn't deal with Jay being in a car crash. I made my way to second period. Each moment I grew more and more nauseous. I asked the teacher for a restroom pass. I needed to be alone in case tears started to fall. I must have looked like hell because she didn't question me.

I sat in the stall doing my breathing and meditation exercises that I practiced every night. I felt calmer, but I couldn't shake the feeling of sorrow deep within me. I needed my mom. Tears filled my eyes, and I leaned my head against the cold, graffiti-filled metal bathroom wall. The bell rang. I had spent most of second period in a bathroom stall. I quickly headed back to the classroom.

As I gathered my things, my teacher approached me, clearly concerned.

"Sweetie, you don't look any better. You better

see the nurse. You look like you're about to come undone."

I nodded and was on my way toward the nurse's office. I'd never had to visit the nurse in my entire high school career. I opened the door and smelled the antiseptic lingering in the air. The nurse was busy typing at her computer.

"I'll be with you in a moment," she said.

I breathed in and out, inflating and deflating my lungs completely. I counted all the cheap knick-knacks the nurse had on her shelf. Thirty-seven ugly porcelain figurines. It reminded me of a garage sale.

"Sorry about your wait." She looked up from the computer and her face dropped when she saw me. "Oh my. What happened? She motioned for me to sit on a cot.

"I don't know. I don't feel well." The panic was growing again.

The nurse checked my vitals and commented on how anxious I appeared. "Sweetheart, we need to slow your breathing down." She guided me through some breathing exercises, but after a few minutes, I wasn't getting any better. "I think it's time to call your mom."

I heard her talking quietly to my mom on the phone. I curled my legs in toward my chest and retreated into my head, drowning in sadness for some unknown reason. Tears had begun falling by the time my mom arrived.

Mom asked, "Brogen, what happened?" I shook my head. I had no answer. "I'm gonna take her home."

"Okay. I just need you to sign her out." The

nurse handed my mom a paper.

My arm began tingling. I squeezed my fist tightly and released it, but the tingles remained. I breathed slower and slower, and the tingles were less intense. So weird. We continued on to the car. I didn't even stop at my locker to get my stuff.

"Brogen, I want to help you, but I don't know what's happening. I need you to talk to me, please." Mom sounded worried.

"I don't know what's wrong." My voice quivered. "I said goodbye to Jay, and I had this overwhelming feeling of sadness take over my body. What the hell is wrong with me?"

"I don't know for sure," Mom said.

"What do you mean?"

"Well, sometimes people who are empathic can sense when something bad is going to happen. I've had it happen a few times in my life. But I can't call it up—the feeling will come on its own, and I sit, helpless, and later find out some bad news. Or maybe you picked up on someone's energy. Let's call Mrs. Taylor to check on Meg, just in case."

Mom dialed her number before we left the school parking lot. I listened to my mom's voice, trying to quiet the sobs wanting to escape me and the nausea tickling the back of my throat. "Are you sure?" She paused to listen to Meg's mom. "Okay, thanks. That's great news." Mom turned to me and said, "She's great. They have her walking around and think she'll go home in two days."

It wasn't Meg. When I thought of Meg, I felt peace and joy. I thought of Becca and felt her ugliness tainting the air, but even Becca's energy didn't feel the same as what I felt inside. I thought of Jay and me in the hall saying goodbye, and my stomach turned.

"Pull over, *now!*" Mom stopped on the shoulder and I pushed out the door and threw up my breakfast. It was Jay. Just thinking of him made me feel like death was in front of me. I began to cry hard. Mom came over and wrapped me in her arms. "It's Jay. Something's gonna happen to him, Mom." I was choking on my sobs.

Mom rocked and shushed me. "We don't know that for sure. I know it feels like it, but we have to wait and see. Let's go home. Not much we can do about this right now. Do you have his phone number?" I shook my head. "Address?" I nodded. I knew where his aunt and uncle lived. "Good. We'll go there later to make sure he is okay. Then you'll feel better. Right now, we need to calm you down."

If anyone else were my mother, I probably would've been locked up in a mental institute. It felt crazy to be overwhelmed with emotion when there was nothing happening to explain it...crazy. Thankfully my mother was empathic *and* a psychologist, so she could relate to me and help me through this. We got back in the car and drove home.

As soon as we got home, Mom made me go for a "getting to know nature" walk. Mom wanted me to focus on the sights, sounds, and smells around me. She wanted to get my mind to focus on something I could see and feel, rather than some invisible energy I couldn't control. It was probably some strategy from her newest psychology textbook. She took me down the street where we cut through a backyard and entered a wooded area. Many of the leaves had fallen from the wind blowing the lifeless foliage. They crunched beneath our feet as we tread across them, breaking into little pieces. A little bird chirped from a high branch; he watched us cautiously. As we neared him, he flew off in fear. Mom asked me to find thirty acorns so she could fill a vase at home. Another distraction, but I was up for it. The ground beneath the oak was covered in acorns, and I stuffed my pockets full. We walked a while longer, and I told Mom I was feeling better.

"Good, you look a little calmer." I knew she was assessing my energy as much as my appearance. She probably sensed the dread settling inside me. "Think you might try some lunch?"

"Yeah. I think I could keep some down," I answered.

Mom filled the rest of my afternoon with mini chores and mental distractions. She never left me alone to stew in my worries. We planned to visit Meg around four o'clock, have a nice dinner out, and then stop by Jay's house.

Meg was a sight for sore eyes. I always felt better around her. She was sitting up in bed working on homework. I couldn't resist teasing her. "Man, homework? They don't let you wait till you're out of the hospital? What a bunch of losers."

Meg laughed and gave me a big hug. "There is no way I am letting this stupid accident hold me back a year. I don't want to be a junior while you are a senior…that is all kinds of wrong."

I chuckled but was glad to see the fight back in

my friend. "Good girl." I didn't dare tell her anything about how bad my day went. I needed Meg to get out of this hospital, and I didn't want to affect her mood.

"So, doc says I can go home tomorrow. I can't wait to sleep in my own bed. And eat junk food in the middle of the night." She beamed.

I laughed. It's funny how you miss the simple things in life when you can't have them. "How is your leg?" I asked.

Meg lifted the covers back. There was a light gauze dressing covering her thigh. "I'll look a little Frankenstein-ish, but I'll be fully functional." Meg and I chatted until Mom came back in the room. She really seemed like her old self.

After getting a much needed hug and saying goodbye to Meg, Mom and I ate a quick meal at the corner taco stand, then we headed to Jay's. The sun had already disappeared for the day since winter was approaching. The streetlamps turned on and cast their golden glow on the passersby below. Jay's house had the lights on, so it was easy to recognize. I hoped Jay was home. I felt fluttery and buzzy inside my body, like I had overdosed on adrenaline.

Mom turned to me. "Want me to go with you?"

I debated this for a moment. I could use her support, but I was a big girl and felt strange going to the door with my mom. "Could you wait for me here in the car? I might be a few minutes."

Mom nodded, then bent over and kissed my cheek. "I love you."

"I love you too."

I walked to the front door and felt so torn inside

my body. Part of me wanted to run away, cower, and never know why I had that terrible feeling. The other part of me stood tall and wanted to understand this. I willed my feet to move forward and managed to ring the bell. After two rings, I heard footsteps.

Soren answered the door. "Brogen, what are you doing here?"

He looked surprised to see me. He was dressed in a baggy t-shirt and some comfy lounge pants, more casual than his usual look at school. But there was more. Something was off. Soren seemed uncomfortable. Something bad had happened, and he wasn't prepared for giving me that news.

"Is Jay here?" I asked.

"Jay, yeah. Listen, he is here, but now is not a good time."

"Is he okay?" I was searching Soren's face for answers.

"Sure. Listen, I'll let him know you came by and ask him to talk to you tomorrow. See ya." Soren shut the door.

Sure? What kind of answer was that? If Jay was hurt, surely he'd say something other than 'sure.' So, at least I knew he was alive, but Soren didn't give anything else away. I walked to the car. My mom was surprised that I was back so soon.

"Well, he's alive. But he couldn't come to the door, so I don't know." I glanced down and noticed my hands were twisting and turning with nerves.

"Well, not much more you can do then. Do you feel any better?" she asked.

"Just a little."

"Listen, don't dwell on it. He's okay. We can

figure the rest out later. Take a hot bath when we get home and hit the sack early. You've got to be exhausted from all that adrenaline."

When we got home I did as Mom suggested. I put on some music, made the water extra hot, and sank deep into the hot tingles the water created all over my skin. I stayed in until the water cooled down. I was sufficiently pruned and needed some cream to replenish my wrinkled-up skin. After brushing my teeth and putting on my pjs, I sketched till I felt the draw of sleep. With the covers pulled under my chin, I closed my eyes and envisioned a fern frond. With each breath the frond uncoiled and recoiled, uncoiled, recoiled, uncoiled...

The next day I made it to school a little early. My locker was as good as new with the artwork removed. I wondered if my breakdown yesterday scared the staff into cleaning it off in record time. I took out my books and walked to Jay's locker. I waited until the bell rang for first period, but there was no Jay, so I went on to class, not caring I was late. I took my seat and glanced across the room. I was surprised to see Jay sitting at his desk. He didn't look up, and he wasn't bantering with the guys around him. He looked off...like there was a black rain cloud over his head.

My teacher cleared his throat. "Nice of you to join us, Miss Mathers. Would you mind opening your book so I may continue?"

I was still looking at Jay. He had not even turned my way.

"Yes, sorry sir," I replied.

I hated being this close to Jay and not being able

to ask if he was okay. I glanced at him several times in class, but unlike before, his eyes never met mine. He was like a turtle hiding in his shell. After class, I gathered my things slowly, hoping to bump into Jay. Unfortunately, this backfired because he bolted out the door. I was beginning to suspect I wouldn't see him at lunch. He was avoiding me. What had changed?

In the lunch line, I saw Soren a few feet ahead of me. I excused myself in line and came up next to him. "Hey, Soren. What the heck is up with Jay? He flew out of first period super-fast."

"I don't know, Brogen, maybe he had to take a leak," he said jokingly. "Listen, it's not my deal, so I can't say anything. If you wanna know what's up with Jay, you're gonna have to ask him yourself. Sorry, not trying to be mean, it's just not my deal to tell."

"Thanks, and sorry to put you in the middle."

Jay never came to lunch, but I did see him later in the day at his locker. I knew there was a swim meet after school, so I called my mom to tell her I was attending it and would be home later. I packed up my bag and went to the restroom before heading to the aquatic building. I grabbed a seat near the floor so I could chat with Jay if the chance arose. But Jay wasn't at the meet. I pulled one of his teammates aside and asked if they knew where he was. The swimmer said Jay quit the team earlier that day. What the heck?

I walked home and found myself alone. Mom had patients tonight, so I heated some leftovers and watched TV. I stared blankly at the screen and searched my mind for what could have happened to Jay. He went for some tests, but he seemed healthy, even swam on the school team. Why would he quit the team? Maybe something happened to his dad? I wished Soren would tell me or Jay would sit still long enough for me to ask him.

Today sucked. Tomorrow had to be better.

***

At school, I was greeted by Becca's taunting voice. "What happened to your boyfriend?"

"Bug off, Becca." I wasn't in the mood for her and did not hesitate letting her know that.

Jay was not in school the rest of the week. I worried he moved away. Maybe his dad came out of rehab and they went home. Maybe he had cancer? School was not the same without Jay. The days dragged on, and I counted minutes to pass the time. At night I couldn't stop my brain from fretting over what was happening. I needed to know. I would deal with whatever it was, but not knowing was going to drive me insane.

"Where are you?" Mom asked me randomly on Thursday.

"Umm, right here."

"Are you okay? You've been spacey all week," she probed.

I nodded. I didn't have any answers.

"If you wanna unload what's on your mind, you know where to find me."

Soon it was Friday…too many days without Jay. I impulsively ditched my last class and went to

Jay's house. Finding Jay and talking with him was worth the detention I'd probably earn. I'd never ditched school before, and while it was exhilarating, it was also a bit terrifying. But, I pulled it off without a problem, probably because no one suspected a rule follower to ditch.

I ran most of the way but slowed when I got to his street. I wasn't sure what I'd say, I just let my feet carry me away. My heart rate picked up when I saw him shooting baskets on his aunt's driveway. I would have to trust my gut and wing the impromptu conversation.

"So, too cool for school? Or did the NBA approach you?"

Jay turned to me, surprised. His cheeks were flushed from the cold and exercise. The shadows under his eyes seemed darker. His face held no joy.

"Sorry, didn't mean to startle you," I said. The wind blew an icy breeze at me just then, and I shivered.

"What are you doing here? School's not out yet," Jay said.

"Actually, I hoped you could help me out." I plopped down on the grass under the basketball net and wrapped my coat around me tightly. "God, how can you stand to be out here without a coat?" The wind blew another bitter gust at me.

"You ditched class to ask me why I'm outside without a coat?" He was irritated.

"No, but it's freezing out here. Sorry." He didn't offer to move to a warmer location, and there was no smile to light up his face. "Anyway, I think I'm going crazy. See, I had the strangest sensation come over me when I said goodbye to you before your doctor's appointment last week." As soon as the sentence finished, I felt anxiety and darkness rolling off of him. He looked away and began dribbling the ball. "I haven't had a chance to ask how that went. Is everything okay?"

"Sure. Why do you care?"

Why did I care? *Because I like you, maybe love you. Because you saved my life. Because you're funny and kind. Because I want you to be okay. Because I felt like someone took my heart and stuck it in a blender.*

"I can't help thinking that my mood was linked to that appointment. I know...sounds crazy. I honestly think so too. But, if something happened, it might explain why I've felt like something awful was going to happen. I feel like a freak losing her mind." I muttered that last part, but he must have heard. He stopped dribbling and approached me. "Please, tell me you're okay," I pleaded.

"If I tell you...I can't take it back."

What an odd thing to say. I nodded in agreement and was now more curious than ever. He sat down on the ball in front of me. For the longest time he stared at me, studying me.

Finally, he stood up and chuckled. "Actually, never mind. I'm teasin'. I'm fine. 100 percent fine." He dribbled the ball away from me and shot a basket. "Go home, Brogen. I'll be back in school Monday."

"Wait." I went up to Jay and grabbed his arm. He looked at it like it burned his skin, so I quickly removed it. "You can tell me, I won't tell." The look in his eyes was full of conflict. There was more to the story than he was letting on. He wanted to tell me, but he couldn't, or wouldn't. "I know something happened."

"I'm good. Go home, Brogen."

He grabbed the ball and headed toward the house without looking back. He turned a cold shoulder to our friendship, and I had no idea why.

At home, I was surprised to see Mom sitting at the kitchen table in a rigid position. She was pissed. I had totally forgotten that I'd ditched.

"Care to tell me why you skipped class?"

Ugh. "Mom, it won't happen again. A friend of mine was in trouble, and I had to talk with them." I conveniently left out the part that mentioned Jay was the friend in need, and I left school grounds to go to his house.

She studied me and read my energy. Her anger slipped away. "Okay, don't do it again. It was nice of you to care for your friend, but I don't approve of choices that negatively impact your life."

I nodded in agreement. I didn't even learn anything new, so my ditch was pointless. Hopefully I would not get a detention slip on Monday.

Chapter 11

"Think Jay will be here today?" Meg asked. I shook my head because I honestly did not know. "Do you still like him?" she prodded. I shrugged my shoulders as I closed my locker and turned around. Jay was a few inches from me, staring as if he overheard us. Meg suspected this too and mouthed the word "sorry," but I wasn't mad at her. Jay shut *me* out. *He* did this to us.

In algebra, Jay sat staring straight ahead. He seemed good, strong, and healthy. I tried to spot what might be different about him, but came up empty...until the bell rang. The girl sitting next to him dropped her books, and Jay bent down to pick them up. I saw a black paracord bracelet with a silver medallion on it strung around his right wrist. This wasn't a big difference, but I had never seen it before, and he wasn't the jewelry wearing type. I hoped to get a closer look at lunch time.

Meg was sitting in our usual spot, and I glanced over at Soren. He was laughing it up with the kids at the table and eating his lunch. Jay walked over and set his tray down. Jay wore his hoodie, which hid the bracelet.

"Hello? Earth to Brogen. Am I not good enough company for you?" Meg interrupted my staring. "What are you looking at anyway?" She followed my gaze to Jay's table, then smiled at me. "Never mind. Your man is back *and* you still like him," she teased.

"He is not my man. Actually, I'm trying to see his bracelet," I added.

"Why, is it super cool? I didn't take Jay as a jewelry wearing kinda guy." Meg popped an apple slice in her mouth. "Listen, in English Lit we are in small groups today. I'll get with his group and check into it."

"Thanks, Meg." We ate and talked about our boring weekend while staring in Jay's direction.

When 3:00 p.m. hit, Meg found me at my locker. "Okay, Jay's bracelet is a medic alert bracelet. No clue as to why he wears one, though. He was kinda weird and withdrawn in class, not like himself. What's his deal?"

I shook my head and packed up my books. "I don't know." Jay was walking several feet in front of us. "I'll talk to you tomorrow. I'm gonna try to catch up to him."

"Good luck," Meg wished.

I picked up my pace, not wanting to appear too obvious. I wasn't in as good of shape as I'd been before the accident, and the cold air hurt my lungs, but I was gaining ground. With just a few feet left, a silver VW Jetta pulled up to Jay. It was Becca and her friends offering a ride. Surprisingly, he got in, even though his aunt's house was only a block and a half away. I stayed far enough back to spy without being spotted and noted they did not turn down Jay's street. What the hell? He avoided me, but jumped into Becca's car. My heart sank. He chose her over me.

The next morning, Becca was hanging all over Jay like syrup on a waffle. He didn't seem repulsed by it; in fact, he even smiled. I tried not to watch, but it was like a car crash on the side of the road—you just had to look. Becca gave Jay a peck on the cheek before heading to class. He gave her a half smile, then turned and caught me staring at him. Heat rushed to my cheeks, and I quickly diverted my eyes. Jay said nothing and walked away with downcast eyes. I had lost him and it hurt.

At lunch he sat with Becca and her crew. I had to turn my chair away from them because the jealousy was eating me up. Meg did her best to distract me and tried to make plans for the weekend. It was mindless chatter, but it filled the half hour. After lunch, I headed to the bathroom. I picked the middle stall and heard some girls come in after me to gossip by the sinks.

"He's so hot. Becca is so lucky," one girl said.

"I heard they went all the way, and Jay was to die for," another said.

My mouth dropped open, and I peered through the bathroom door to see who was talking. It was a wannabe group that followed the Blonde-squad. I flushed the toilet and went to wash my hands. One of them shushed the others.

"Hey, Brogen," a little brunette said.

I didn't know her name, but I knew she was in first period with Jay and me. I nodded in her direction and left the bathroom. When I hit the hall I heard laughter coming from the bathroom behind me. I was pissed. Screw Jay. Screw Becca. I wanted my life to go back to normal. I wanted it to be Meg and me cruising through our junior year, mostly unrecognized and totally drama-free. Interacting with Jay bought me a ticket into the world of social hell, and I didn't want to be there. He would hear it from me today. I wanted off this ride.

When the final bell rang, I grabbed my stuff and ran for the school doors. I was going to catch Jay before Becca and her gang swooped him up in her car. I waited at the bottom of the stairs, trying to look calm. Everyone left through this door, so I was guaranteed to see him. Soren passed me and said a quick, "Hey, Brogen." I worried about what would happen if Becca came out first, or if they came out together. I hadn't thought about what I would do then…abort the mission? God, it was freezing outside. The clouds were heavy with precipitation. Maybe we would see snow before Thanksgiving. I scanned the crowd at the top of the stairs and found Jay bounding down the steps. When he hit the last one I picked up my bag and caught up to him.

"Jay, wait. I need to talk to you." He had the nerve to roll his eyes at me, but he stopped and faced me.

"Fine, what do you want?"

I would be lying if I said his coldness didn't piss me off and hurt. "Five minutes."

"Fine." He led me to an alcove away from the

exiting students. "What?"

"What has happened? What happened to *us*? I had a normal life—quiet, one amazing friend, no drama—before you came to town." I licked my lips. He stared down at me, prepared to take whatever I gave him…his walls were up. "Then you show up, save my life, and shower me with kindness and charisma." A tear fell down my face. "I let you in." I looked down at the ground and tried to gather the strength in my voice to say the next part. "I never let anyone in." I lost myself as the realization set in. "Then, as fast as you drew me in, you pushed me away. And now? Here I am…without you and drowning in drama." I peered up at him and he stared at me intently, but he was silent. "I was willing to take the drama, any and all of it, if I had you. But you've turned away from me, and…chose Becca. I can't believe you slept with her." I had to look away when I said that last part. "I want off the merry-go-round. I'm sick of it. I'm sick of hoping you'll be my friend again, only to find out you have nothing to say to me." I shook my head. More tears. "That's it. You can't have any more of me." I turned and walked away from him.

He didn't follow. I left him standing there with a shocked look on his face. I put on my sunglasses so I didn't have to worry about the tears falling from my eyes. When I was ten steps away, I heard Becca in a group of girls gushing over Jay and bragging she was going to ask him to come home with her again. Bitch.

Chapter 12

"Brogen, are you okay?" Meg called my phone as soon as I got home.

"No. I couldn't keep my shit together to find out why he's been blowing me off. Instead, I told him I want out of his life." I was still mad.

"I know, he told me."

"Wait, you talked to him? What the hell?" I couldn't believe Meg and Jay spoke. I was sure Jay and Becca were going to head to her lair for a romp in the sack after school.

"Well, he kinda found me on the walk home. He seemed pretty frustrated. I gave him your number."

"You *what*? Why did you do that?" I demanded.

"I don't know. He wanted your address, and I didn't think you'd want to see him. Plus, he's annoyingly persistent. I made him settle for your number."

I sighed. I didn't think I could face him again.

Meg sounded remorseful. "Brogen, I'm sorry. He said you were upset. What happened between you two? What did you say to him? You two were

97

so tight after he saved you. I thought you wanted to see if you guys could work things out."

This was so hard because I did want to work things out. "I know, but Becca...I can't compete. I'm not in her league."

Meg clucked her tongue. "Listen, do me a favor. If he calls you, keep an open mind and listen to him. I don't think he wants to lose you."

"Then why does he keep pushing me away and running to Becca?"

"He doesn't give a crap about Becca. Do they seem close to you? Do you think he has confided in her and not you?"

"No," I said in a small voice. I hadn't thought about it like that. Whatever was going on between Becca and Jay was strictly physical, anyone could see that. She may have wanted more, but he didn't seem to share that with her. I let out a long sigh. "Fine, I'll be open minded."

Meg and I hung up. My phone fell from my hands onto the ground. I kicked it away with my foot out of frustration, and it landed next to my drawing journal. I felt compelled to thumb through the journal before I finished it, to break my rules. Page one was dated June 5. It was black and white, with pictures of various birds. Some were on branches, others had taken flight in the sky. I rifled through countless drawings throughout the summer timeframe, all very peaceful. Many were of plants, flowers, and tiny insects. There were occasional sayings or poems written in the margin. All black and white. As school approached, my sketches were drawn with a heavier, bolder line and seemed more anxious. How fitting. I continued thumbing through and found a page with a colorful butterfly. Everything else was black and white, but the butterfly was so vivid. I checked the date. It was the day I returned to school after the accident—the day Jay had kissed me, the day we had lunch together. I turned page after page, and the subsequent entries each had color on them. All of them. I gasped and the journal fell to the floor.

I never consciously decided which pencil to draw with. I walked over to my desk, the place where I mindlessly let my emotions out on paper each night. The old canning jar that sat at the corner of the desk was filled with over twenty colored pencils and several lead pencils. Could the accident have changed me, or was this Jay's influence? I grabbed the book again and thumbed to the last few entries. They still had color in them, but there was more black and white. I looked for the day Jay went to the doctor and I had the panic attack...black, black, black. Scribbling and chaos. It wasn't the accident. It was Jay. Somehow I tuned into his energy and it came through in my drawings. I couldn't believe the difference in what I'd drawn. I thought I had better control of shielding myself, but instead I was attuned to Jay's issues. I was pulled from my thoughts by my phone ringing. "Unknown number." I took a deep breath, tucked my journal in my bedside table, and answered my phone.

"Hello?" There was a pause.

"Brogen, don't hang up." It was Jay. "Listen, I need to talk to you. Can I come over?" I didn't want to see him. It's easier to push someone away on the phone. "Please, I promise I'll explain what's been going on. But I need to do it in person."

I desperately wanted to know what had changed our relationship, but my heart begged for a reprieve from sadness. Did I want him to confess he was in love with Becca to my face? It might crush me. Unfortunately, my mouth betrayed me and rattled off my address. Jay didn't even say goodbye, he just hung up.

Seven minutes later, the doorbell rang. Jay's cheeks were pink from the frigid air, and he was hopping about to keep warm. I didn't invite him inside.

"Thanks for letting me come over."

This was not some playdate. I wanted him to get on with it and get out of here...let me get on with my life. "What did you want to say?" No pussyfooting around.

He rubbed his hand through his hair, contemplating how to word his speech. "I guess the most important thing I need you to know is that I'm sorry. I never wanted to drag you into drama. I never meant to hurt you. Honestly. When I put the letter in the mailbox that night, and heard the dog growling at you, I wanted to help." He shook his head like it was a mistake he couldn't seem to get rid of. "I didn't think about what would happen between us. That dog was gonna attack. I had to help."

Hearing Jay reflect back on that night made me feel bad for snapping and turning my back on him. He had saved me, and for that I'd always be grateful.

"Come in. You'll catch your death out there."

Jay gave a half smile and stepped inside. He kicked off his shoes and shrugged off his coat. I motioned for him to sit on one end of the couch while I sat opposite him. I didn't say anything to him. The silence was deafening.

"I can't really tell you what's going on. Not yet. I'm trying to figure some stuff out." He leaned forward and shoved his hands into his hair in frustration.

"I wish you could tell me. It's frustrating to see you bothered by something and not know what it is."

"I'm sorry. I just feel like my life is a runaway train barreling toward a cliff. I have no control and it's gonna end in disaster." His expression was sad.

"At least you have Becca to lean on." *Ladies and Gentlemen, the nice version of Brogen is taking a timeout while the Bitch has been unleashed.* "I bet she's great at making guys forget their problems." I crossed my arms over my chest. Defensive body language. I couldn't help it.

He turned to me in shock. "What the hell, Brogen? Are you jealous, or just a bitch?" He waited for an answer, but I think he already knew it. He squared his shoulders and faced me. "First, it's none of your business what happens between Becca and me. You and me…honestly, I don't know what we are. Friends? Damsel in distress and knight in shining armor? Classmates? Nothing?" That last one stung. It was a suggestion, but it hit me hard. "I don't know. I'm not sure about anything anymore. Not sure why I'm here." The last words were said so quietly. He stood and walked to the door. "So, I'm really sorry you got pulled into all of this. I never meant for you to get hurt. Probably best to keep your distance from me because I'm not sure it's over yet." He opened the door and left without looking back.

I sat on the couch unable to move. My heart hurt and I felt the tears falling down. Mom was beside me suddenly. We sat in silence and she stroked my hair.

After the tears stopped falling, Mom broke the silence. "Who was that boy, and what was he doing here?"

"Wait. Why are you home? I mean, aren't you supposed to be with patients?"

"Cancellations. Now, tell me about that boy," Mom said.

"That's Jay. Remember? Rabid dog party Jay. He basically exited my life tonight." I looked up at my mom and she seemed spooked. "What? Why do you look like that?"

"I didn't realize that was *the* Jay, the one who saved you. And what do you mean he exited your life?"

"He said his life is going crazy right now and he's really confused. I tried to reach out to him, but he pushed me away and turned to Becca. I thought we had a connection. I let him in." The sobs began and Mom held me tight.

"I'm so sorry, sweetie."

I was ready for one of her psychology-based lectures on emotions and teen boys, but it never came. "What? No ten minute lecture on guys?

What's going on?" I wiped the tears away and faced my mom. She looked like she was holding her tongue. "Come on, Mom. No secrets."

She sighed and then asked, "Has Jay told you anything about his life?"

"Umm, a little. I know why he's living with his aunt and uncle. Why?" Mom shifted uneasily in her chair. "What's this about? You're kind of freakin' me out."

"Jay started coming to me as a patient a few weeks ago. You are *not* to repeat this." She waited for me to nod. "He has a lot that he's dealing with, more than any teen should have to deal with."

I looked at Mom, waiting for her to spill the beans, but she was silent again. "*Mom!* You can't bait me with that and leave me hanging."

"I can't tell you, honey. It's his right to privacy. It's his story to tell. Telling you he's my patient was already too much."

"I won't tell, you know that." It was true. I was a trustworthy kid. If I said it, I meant it.

"I do. And because I know that *and* because I know what kind of person you are, I think you need to be a friend to him now more than ever."

My eyes met hers, and mine were filling with tears again. "He doesn't want me, Mom. Besides, he has Becca and his cousin. He came over to apologize and leave my life." Mom was shaking her head. Why did she want this? Didn't she realize how painful it would be for me? I didn't want to be rejected. I didn't want the drama. "Mom, what the hell? Don't use me as a pawn in your therapy."

"Brogen, I'm not. You are empathic, kind and

bright, and an amazing friend. I couldn't pick a better person to be in Jay's life right now. And just because he said those things, I'm gonna bet that he'd appreciate you being in his life, in whatever way you are capable. You, Brogen, have the gift to make Jay's life a little brighter during this hard time."

"Boy, you'd make a great greeting card writer." How could I say no to that? "Okay, I'll try. No promises, though, and be prepared to pick up the broken pieces of my heart."

"Good girl. I love you." Mom planted a kiss on my head.

I was grateful my mom was still alive to reassure me and kiss me when I needed it. Jay's mom was no longer around to do those things for him. I bet it was hard not having that parental support when things were tough.

Chapter 13

Sitting in my old four-door car, I pondered how I could convince Jay to have a coffee with me. Fifteen minutes later, I managed to start my car and drive to Jay's house. I needed to get brave fast. I fidgeted with the stereo in hopes of finding something loud and angry on the radio. As I adjusted the volume, there was a tapping on my driver's side window. Jay was standing next to my car with the newspaper in hand. Busted. He was breathtaking in his sweats and t-shirt. I rolled down the window.

"Hey, sexy paperboy. Come have a coffee with me." Ack! I sounded ridiculous...so out of my element.

His eyebrows raised straight up at this. He paused a moment to consider his move. "You have a thing for paperboys, huh?"

"Maybe. Seriously, come have a coffee with me," I repeated.

He looked down at the paper in his hands. "Boy, you are forward today. I'm not used to a girl taking the first step." He smiled. "It's kinda hot."

"Come on. I promise I won't keep you long."

He hesitated, debating whether he should come with me. Then he jogged up to the front of the house, tossed the paper in, and shouted something into the house. He climbed into the passenger seat a minute later.

"So, since you are asking *me* out, does that mean you are treating?"

I turned to him and smiled. "Absolutely."

I felt the zings in my chest from being in close proximity to him. He was gorgeous. He had strong cheekbones, and the slight shadowing under his eyes made the hazel color of his irises more brilliant.

"Mind if I adjust the heat? It's kinda cold out," he asked.

I shook my head. The warm air blew his scent my way. It reminded me of a fresh breeze on a sunny day.

The local coffee joint was only five minutes from Jay's house. The cozy, rustic shop had wood floors, brick accents, mustard-yellow walls lined with indie artists' paintings, and comfy nooks to cuddle in. It was the perfect backdrop to the most divine smell of fresh brewed coffee. Jay and I ordered drinks and a pastry, and I was good to my word and treated him. We sat in a quiet corner where two comfy chairs resided with a side table between them.

"So," I began, "I like having you in my life. We were kind of thrown together thanks to Cujo, but I do *not* believe I like you because I feel indebted to you." He listened to me intently. "I've decided, you may not exit my life…not gonna happen." I shook my head. "I don't care if Becca and you are an item. I will tolerate the drama."

"Wait, wait, wait…what's changed? I thought you were done," he asked. He appeared hopeful, but cautious.

Good question. How should I phrase this? My mom says you need a good friend? I still like you? I have multiple personalities and that was my evil personality coming out?

"It hurt too much to have you walk away the other night. You've become a big part of my life. I don't know what happened to make things go sour between us, but I need us to at least be friends. I need you in my life."

He grinned from ear to ear. "God, I'm so damn happy you said that. It killed me to think that crap was happening to you because of knowing me. And…my life kinda sucks without you too. Life is so complicated. Some days it takes everything just to get out of bed. I started seeing a shrink to try and help me keep my head straight. Can you believe that?" He shook his head as if he couldn't believe it, but I could, because I already knew this.

"Is it helping?" I asked.

"I think so. I probably wouldn't be back at school if it wasn't. My aunt made me go after I refused to attend school that one week. The shrink seems nice, she's like my mom's age, or what she would have been if she was still alive."

I felt bad that Jay was missing his mom. "That must be so hard to not have your mom around."

"Yeah...or Dad," he reminded me.

That was a lot to handle. I nodded and placed my hand over his knee. "Sorry, Jay."

"The shrink is gonna help me break some news to my dad. I'm not sure what he'll do when he hears it. I'm hoping he's strong enough, but I'm afraid it might challenge his sobriety. We meet next week." Jay rubbed his hands through his hair. "I'm scared. I don't want to lose him. I need him now more than ever, but he became a broken man when my mom passed." I listened. I had no idea what he was going through. I had my mom's warm arms to wrap around me when times got tough, and I couldn't care less about my dad. "The shrink keeps telling me how I'm dealing with a lifetime of drama within a short time. But, I don't want this. I didn't choose this. Friggin' sucks," Jay added.

"No, you didn't choose it. Hopefully the other people in your life are supportive and can help fill in the gaps when needed." I patted his knee. "I promise I'll be here for you if you ever need me."

"No offense, Brogen, but I hate leaning on others. Hate it. I had a great life, and then Mom died and it all changed. Thank you, though, for offering me your support." He took a drink from his mug. "And for the coffee."

"Anything for a sexy paperboy." I may have joked about his sexiness, though he *was* sexy, but I'd be happy to have our friendship back. "Let's get out of here."

Jay and I walked toward the car. The conversation back to his house was light and fun. He seemed like his old self.

"I had a lot of fun. You'll have to treat me to coffee again sometime," he teased.

"You can ask me too. The door swings both ways, buddy."

Jay winked at me and gave me a hug. I waved and put the car in reverse. This was a huge, positive step in the rekindling of our friendship.

At home, I found Mom on the couch watching a comedy on Netflix and knitting a blanket. She seemed eager for news on how it went. I took off my jacket, sat on the couch next to her, and began watching the movie, acting as if nothing important happened today.

She nudged me hard. "Spill it! You'll drive me mad with curiosity."

I laughed and said, "Sorry, patient-doctor confidentiality."

"Ugh!"

"All right, all right." I told my mom some of the details. She seemed pleased with what I told her and didn't push me further.

"It appears this friendship is not just something *he* needs, but you as well. You seem so much happier," my mom said.

I felt happier. I needed to make us work. Jay changed me, and I was better off with him in my life. And if drama was the fee I needed to pay, then I guess I had to pay up.

That night, I stored my sketch journal and brought out a new one. I usually filled every page before starting a new one, but since I cheated and looked at the pages, I didn't feel right continuing in it. Besides, Jay and I were having a fresh start.

What better way to document it than with a fresh sketch journal?

Monday morning, I told Meg all about my weekend and she couldn't stop grinning.

"So, how are you going to manage this with Becca? I mean, she's a bit territorial. The shit's gonna fly."

I laughed at Meg's saying. "I haven't thought that far ahead." I opened my locker and a folded note slipped out.

- Brogen,
Coffee was awesome, pastry was great. But the company was even better. Thursday for a repeat?
- S.P.
Text me.

"Who the flip is S.P.?" Meg asked.

"I think it's Jay, but I don't get the S.P. part." I folded it up and shoved the note in my back jeans pocket. "Ha! Just got it. S.P. Sexy paperboy." Meg was puzzled. "I'll explain at lunch."

We parted ways for first period. I was one of the first to arrive in algebra, so I took my usual seat in the back corner of the room. I took out my phone and began searching the calendar to see if Thursday was open for coffee.

"This seat taken?" I shook my head, not looking up. The teacher entered and ordered all phones to be stored away. "Can I borrow a pencil?" the same voice asked. I handed my pencil to the voice while finding Thursday. I was free. "Sorry again, can I borrow some paper?"

110

"Yeah, but honestly, come to class with your stuff next time." I turned to see Jay sitting there with a big smile on his face, waiting for a piece of paper. "What are you doing here? Your spot is over there," I reminded him.

"I know. Kinda don't care about assigned seats today. Feels pretty freakin' liberating."

I chuckled and passed him the paper. "No chewing or sucking on my pencil."

"Brogen, does math always make you talk dirty?" He winked and I gave him a small shove.

I laughed him off. The teacher took roll and made no remark of Jay sitting in a different seat. Unfortunately, Jay's close proximity meant I didn't get much out of class, because he passed notes with me most of the hour. Most of our notes were friendly banter, but I did agree to the Thursday coffee. When Jay was busy writing, I tried to get a better read on his medic alert bracelet. All I could make out was, "Fragile: Treat as Trauma." I couldn't get the right angle to see the rest. After class, Jay continued bantering with me all the way to my locker. Feeling eyes on me, I turned and saw Becca glaring. I knew Becca did not miss any of Jay's purposeful actions, and I'd be the one to pay for it.

Chapter 14

Thursday could not come fast enough. I was anxious to have coffee after school. Meg wished she could be a fly on the wall at the coffee shop.

"We're just friends. Nothing more," I assured her. Meg rolled her eyes. "Sorry, sweetie. Next coffee date will be me and you though. See ya."

I walked toward the parking lot. Jay had borrowed his aunt's car and told me to meet at the green Honda Accord. As I approached, I heard Jay arguing with Becca.

"We are just friends. It's only coffee. And you know what? You don't own me."

I stopped to give them time to finish. I didn't like Becca, Jay deserved better, but they both looked kind of miserable.

"I can't believe you said that. It's not about owning, it's about respect. I thought we had something," Becca said as she pushed her hands against Jay's chest. I decided to walk up to them.

"We can skip it," I offered.

"You! Why are you trying to snake your way

into this?" Becca turned her evil eyes on me.

"I'm not. I'm not trying to be anything more than a friend. We were just going to have coffee."

"There's no such thing as friends between guys and girls." Maybe Becca had watched too many chick flicks.

"Honestly, Becca, I'm trying to be a friend."

"Why does he need to talk to you when he can talk to me?" She was seething.

That question was not for me to answer. I turned toward Jay. He casually leaned against the car. None of this bothered him. Becca was like a buzzing fly, and he was trying to swat her away so he could get on with his day.

"We're going for coffee, get in, Brogen." He opened the car door and sat down. "I'll call you tonight, and we'll discuss this later," he said to Becca.

I hesitantly got in the car. If Becca were a bomb, she would have exploded just then. Jay put the car in reverse, looking over his shoulder at a frustrated Becca.

"Sorry about that," he said.

"It's ok...to be expected."

Jay looked over at me. "I didn't expect it. We are not boyfriend and girlfriend."

I couldn't believe my ears. "I'm not sure she feels the same way as you." Once we had our drinks, we found a cozy booth to settle in. "I thought you and Becca were together. Even heard you slept with her."

He choked on his coffee and held up his hand to halt the questions. "When you didn't show for the dance, I thought you rejected me. I was pretty bummed and had my own pity party at the dance." I was trying to imagine sad Jay at the dance and felt bad for him. "Becca saw me. She danced with me most of the night till she said she 'needed air.'" He took a sip of his drink and adjusted himself in the booth. "She didn't want to go outside alone, so she asked me to come with to 'protect her.'" He shook his head, as if he didn't want to remember the next part. "We kissed, and she tried to take it further." He studied me, trying to read my emotions. He didn't add anything else.

"Well?" I asked.

"It went a little further, but I'm not into her. It didn't feel right. I made up some excuse and headed back into the dance. We danced some more, but that's it. I made a mistake, sent mixed signals, and now she thinks we're together."

I raised my eyebrow. "And what about after school? You know, that time when she picked you up near your aunt's house?"

"Are you stalking me? How do you know about that?"

I shrugged my shoulders. "I guess I was in the right place at the right time."

"Uh huh." He eyed me suspiciously. "I'm not sure I need to answer that question."

"You know, whatever you did or didn't do with her, she clearly has feelings for you. And if you aren't wanting to take it further, well, it's only gonna get worse the longer you drag it out," I advised.

"I know. It's just, I can't even think about Becca

right now. My mind is racing with seeing my dad. One thing at a time, you know?"

I nodded. "Right, your dad. How's it going?" He shrugged. "How did you find your shrink?" I wondered if Jay knew my mom was his psychologist.

"My doc referred me. She's great. I'm not sure I could handle this as well as I am without her." I knew exactly what he meant. My mom was amazing. I was glad she was in Jay's corner. "Do you think it's weird I see a shrink?" he asked.

"No, not at all." I sipped my coffee. "Actually, the world would be a better place if everyone saw a shrink." I laughed.

"Yeah, true. I felt self-conscious about it at first…made sure no one I knew was in the parking lot before I headed in. But now, I couldn't care less. I'd be lost without her help," he said as he took another sip.

"Seems you've grown up a lot this year. I can't believe it's halfway over." I looked at Jay. He had a faraway look in his eyes.

"Yeah, not sure if I'll stay at Stanton next year or head home with my dad."

Oh man, I hadn't considered that. "Could you stay with Soren if your dad gets out?" I asked.

"I haven't asked them. They've already helped so much, I'd feel bad asking." I nodded, privately hoping he would stay at Stanton. He glanced at his watch. "Listen, I better take you home. I have homework to finish." We stood and cleaned up our table.

"Thanks for the coffee," I said. He turned and

smiled as he got in the car. The remaining daylight was quickly fading, and the streetlamps and house lights were turning on. As we pulled up to my house, my mom walked out toward the backyard. Phew, that was close. I needed to say goodbye before Jay and my mom saw each other.

"You're welcome. I'm glad you said yes to coffee."

I put my hand on the door handle and looked up to see my mom with the garbage bins, walking to the curb. I silently prayed Jay was too distracted with his thoughts to notice my mom. He would feel so betrayed to learn his shrink was my mom.

As I grabbed my purse and pulled the handle...*crash*. Mom dumped a garbage bin on the ground and released a slew of profanities. We both turned in her direction. Jay saw my mom, and I could see in his eyes that the jig was up.

"That's your mom?" His face showed what I feared. Betrayal. "Is that why you were being so chummy? She made you do this?"

In a flash, he lost respect for my mom and me. What should I say? How could I make it right? "Yes, that's my mom. I knew you were her patient, but I don't know anything else." I couldn't look him in the eye any longer. I felt terrible. I wished I could rewind to earlier in the evening and just tell him what I knew. Surely he would have taken it better than he was now.

"I don't believe you." He was so mad. "You pity me. Is that the only reason you want to be my friend?" He shook his head in disgust. "Unbelievable."

"Pity you, for what? Because your mom died and your dad has a drinking problem?" I felt defensive and couldn't help arguing. "I hate that you have a crappy past, but you're almost eighteen, smart, and have great future ahead of you. I think you'll be fine, and I don't feel pity about it," I yelled back.

"And what about the goddamn disorder that probably killed my mom? The one running through my veins? How much time do I have left before it kills me? 'Great future' B.S.!" He was red in the face.

"What?" I asked Jay. "I don't know what you're talking about," I said quietly.

"Bull!" He hit the steering wheel and stared straight ahead.

My heart was pounding in my chest. It was so loud it was hard to think. Mom had finished picking up the trash and hadn't noticed us. Her figure was a retreating shadow.

"I don't know what you are talking about, honest." Neither of us said anything for a bit. "Is that what your bracelet is about?" I asked.

He lifted his hand and studied it in disgust. Then he extended his arm so I could read the inscription.

Fragile: Treat as Trauma
Vascular Ehlers Danlos Syndrome
Type O+
Blood vessels and hollow organs fragile
Call 911

"I've never heard of that before," was all I could think to say. I didn't know what Vascular Ehlers Danlos Syndrome was, and probably wouldn't remember it to look it up. "Was this what your mom died from?" I felt dread and fear creeping up on me. Jay's eyes were sad and empty. My heart was thundering in my chest, and I felt tingly. I tried to breathe calmly and think of something reassuring to say. "Can I look it up? I mean, will you write it down for me so I can look it up?"

He nodded, then sat up straighter and turned to face me. "Um, you don't look so good. Are you all right?" His voice changed from anger and frustration to concern. My vision was darkening. "Brogen, what the hell?"

I could hear the sounds around me. A car door opening. Shouts. I could feel things—the cold breeze, being lifted into the air, and then being placed on a soft surface. The numbness overcoming my body was paralyzing. I heard murmurs and my heart sloshing blood through me. My lungs, rising and falling.

Chapter 15

I woke up on the couch. The TV was on, and Jay was sitting in the nearby chair, watching it with his hand holding mine. My mom paced in the kitchen. I let out a yawn, and Jay turned to me.

"She's up," he called to my mom.

"It happened again, didn't it?" I asked, then he shushed me. Mom came around with orange juice and some crackers.

"You had another panic attack," Mom informed me. "Jay brought you in and wanted to stay till you came out of it."

I felt so embarrassed he witnessed me freaking out like that. "Sorry," I said to Jay.

"God, you scared me so bad. I didn't know what was happening to you. You got real pale and your eyes rolled back, then you passed out."

"I'm okay. I feel rotten, but I'll be fine."

Jay stayed a little longer and helped my mom in the kitchen. I think it was an excuse for them to talk. When he left he kissed my forehead.

"Are you still mad at me?" I asked.

"I left the disorder name with your mom. She and I agree you should read about it with one of us present to make sure you don't have another attack." I didn't miss the fact that he avoided my question, but his kiss and care must've meant he didn't totally hate me.

"That bad huh?" I was half joking.

"Yeah. You're a lightweight. Just promise me you'll agree."

I nodded. "Thanks for helping me tonight."

He kissed my head again and said goodnight. Mom saw him out the door and then came to sit with me on the couch. She lifted my legs onto her lap. Neither of us said anything. Mom rubbed my calves while I closed my eyes and leaned back against the comfy pillow.

"I hate feeling so weak. I hate that I have panic attacks and become a mess. Jay has so much more to deal with, and he's holding it together better than I am."

"Being a teenager is hard enough. You're doing an amazing job. Life gets hard. You just have to learn how to handle those hard moments. You'll get there." I gave a nod in understanding. "And Jay has had his low points, especially with losing his mom and the diagnosis. But he's also learning what to do, and it's becoming more bearable."

"Mom, can you tell me about his disorder before he sees his dad this weekend? I want to know about it so I can support him," I asked.

"Maybe tomorrow, let's see how you are doing. I wanna make sure you are far enough out of this panic attack before adding stress to you. You really care about him," she added.

"I really do. Mom, he felt so betrayed when he saw you. It broke my heart. I feel awful doing that to him. I should have told him my mom was his shrink."

"I know, he and I talked. He felt better when my story matched yours. I told him I could recommend another therapist but he refused it. I think he just needed time to consider it all." Mom stood and held her hand out to me. "Let's get you to bed so you can rest before school." Mom helped me up and I crawled into bed with my clothes on. I had no energy or care to change into pjs. She tucked me in and kissed me goodnight. "I love you," she said before turning out the light.

"I love you too, Mom."

Chapter 16

Jay sat next to me in algebra class again and asked how I was feeling. I assured him I was better. We didn't say much more. I felt pretty ashamed of my panic attack the night before, and pretty low about betraying him. He probably thought I was an emotional head-case.

Lunch was just Meg and me at the table with our nameless tablemates.

"What's up? You seem off today." Meg could see through me and knew when something was up. "Did something happen at the coffee date?"

I didn't want to tell Meg about Jay. It was so complicated, and despite that, it was his story to tell. "Coffee was great. We talked." I glanced over at his table, and Jay was in the middle of telling a funny tale to Soren and the track guys. But he looked up, caught my eye, and gave a half smile.

"So, what? Just friends?"

I shrugged in response. "For now, just friends."

"Damn shame." Meg began telling me something, but I was only half listening. "You sure nothing else is bugging you? Oops, there goes Becca to move in on him again."

I watched Becca in her high heels and tight shirt trot over to Jay's table. She flashed her smile and flipped her hair. Who did that stuff? And who wore heels to high school? I assessed my outfit for the day—tight leggings, flats, and a flowy, geometric print tunic. Even though I was stylish, I wasn't in the same league as Becca. I wondered if Jay and Becca worked things out after yesterday's parking lot incident.

"It seems she's changed guys...she's all over Soren," Meg announced, and sure enough, Becca walked right past Jay and sat by Soren. Meg was staring at me now.

"What? I don't know what the heck is going on over there. Listen, she was upset that Jay and I were having coffee, and he basically said she had no right to be upset, that they weren't an item."

Meg's mouth dropped open. "But I thought they did *it*." I shrugged, not knowing if they had sex or not. "That's *huge*," she said.

"Whatever, I didn't think too much of it, because he was going to call her later. I figured they'd talk it out and be back to normal." I crunched my apple, trying not to gag as Becca swooned over Soren. I half expected Jay to be jealous or sad that Becca was moving in on Soren, but instead he looked up, as if he sensed me, and smiled. I smiled back, then dropped my gaze when I felt myself blushing. "Though, Jay seems pretty okay with Becca moving on."

Jay and I didn't see each other after lunch. I'd

hoped I could wish him luck with his dad tomorrow, but it just didn't happen.

***

Mom was at home and had a snack ready for me when I hit the door.

"Hey, kiddo, how was school?"

"It was school, Mom. Nothing new."

"How are you feeling? Any better?" I nodded while I swallowed my bite of yogurt. "Good. I was thinking you and I could take a walk and talk about Jay. It's pretty warm out."

"Okay." I was anxious to understand his disorder, but afraid too. I was afraid I would look at him differently, or hear something I couldn't bear. I threw my trash away and drank a glass of water while Mom got ready.

She led us toward the community park. It had several play areas, a baseball field, a gazebo, and a walking trail following the river that ran through town. The leaves hadn't grown in on the branches, but the days were growing warmer. It had been a snowless winter and people grew tired of looking at the dead landscape. At least if there had been snow, people would've been excited about the change in scenery, and the kids would fill our town with snowmen of various shapes and sizes. But this year brought none of that, just a lifeless setting of brown grass, stark trees, and not a flower in sight.

"So, I guess I thought we'd be sitting in front of a computer while talking about this," I stated.

"Life lesson number one. Google can be

overwhelming. It also can paint the rosiest and the darkest picture. I researched it after Jay came to me, and I decided that I want to be the one to tell you, not Google. Google can help you with information *after* I talk to you," my mom said. I Googled everything I ever needed help on, but I knew she was right. There was so much information on Google, both good and bad, you had to know how to sift through it. "First, tell me what Jay has told you, or what you already know."

"Umm, not much. I know he had a blood test. He wears a medic alert bracelet that says he's fragile and is to be treated as a trauma patient. Umm, he loved swimming but had to quit the swim team. He had a hard time healing from the dog attack. But, he looks like a healthy kid."

Mom nodded. She was glad to get my puzzle pieces so she knew how to present the info to complete the picture. We walked for minutes or hours, and the sky grew dimmer. Mom talked about body parts and functions, and all the other medical mumbo jumbo. It was hard for me to imagine Jay having these issues.

"So, his mom probably had it since she died at a young age of an aneurysm," Mom concluded.

"God, now he has to tell his dad all of this? His dad lost his wife to this, now his son has the same thing? No wonder Jay is nervous about talking to him. Is there a cure for it? Or a pill to make it better?"

Mom gently shook her head. "No cure, not yet. Maybe not even in his lifetime. But he has the gift of knowledge. Now that he knows what's going on with his body, he can make smarter choices and do things the doctors think might help prevent issues vEDS patients often face." I felt my heart beating faster. "Breathe, Brogen."

"I'm not sure learning you have a potential fatal disorder is a gift," I said.

"Seems strange, I agree. But you'll see for yourself in time."

"I don't even know what to do with all this information, Mom. Does he know all of this?"

"Yes. I'm impressed at his level-headedness and his drive to want to live a long and full life. If he can keep his head, he'll live life a little fuller and make more memories because he won't take life for granted. I take life for granted all the time. I get caught up in the day to day routine and forget to make time to create new memories with you." Mom side hugged me.

She had an interesting point. I was so used to grumbling about high school drama, which didn't seem to matter now, and I had stopped taking a moment to smell the roses. Instead, I stomped past them, dwelling on petty things.

"So how do you feel about it all?" she asked.

I raised my eyebrows and let out a long breath. "It sucks. I mean, *really* sucks. I feel so bad for him. His life is like a soap opera, almost unreal."

"I know. No kid should have to go through all that he has. But he doesn't want pity. He wants to live a happy life for as long as he can. But Brogen, you cannot share this with anyone. No one." I nodded in agreement. "We better head back. I need to do a few things before tomorrow."

We walked on the tree-lined path back to the house. Squirrels chased each other in a nearby tree, frolicking about without a care in the world. Mom unlocked the back door and we washed up before starting dinner.

We ate dinner in silence, both lost in our own thoughts, and didn't say much more before parting ways at bedtime. I brushed my teeth and got ready for bed. I noticed my message light was blinking on my phone. It was Jay.

Jay: Hey, you still awake?

Me: Yeah, what's up?

Jay: Just listening to some music. Did you talk to your mom yet?

I wasn't sure how to best answer that.

Me: Yes.

There was a long pause before he wrote more.

Jay: Do you wish you never met me?

Me: What?! No. Why would you think that?

Jay: Just wondered if you got scared off. I'm kinda used to people running when things get tough. Listen, I could use a distraction tomorrow evening, a reward for facing my dad. Are you available for a movie?

Me: Yes of course. Just tell me when and who's driving.

Jay agreed and promised to text me tomorrow when the meeting finished. I then wished him luck and said goodnight. I grabbed my sketch journal and drew until I felt sleepy. I filled three pages, the most I had ever completed in one night. I turned out my light, left my room, and climbed into bed with Mom. She normally stayed up later to watch the news, but she was heading to see Jay's dad with Jay, his Aunt, and Uncle in the morning.

"Are you still awake?" I asked as I cuddled against my mom's back.

"Yes. You okay?" She turned to face me, probably to read my emotions, which would be hard to do in the dark.

"Just...nauseous. I've been doing great with others' emotions. In fact, I almost thought I wasn't empathic anymore." Mom reached over and brushed a hair back on my head. "But this stuff with Jay is so heavy. It's..."

"I know, baby."

"I'm worried about tomorrow. He asked me to see a movie with him afterward."

"Don't forget I will be there supporting him. I'll make sure tomorrow is not a total mess. And I'm proud of him for thinking of a nice reward to end the day," she remarked.

"Why aren't you trying to shelter me and keep me from interacting with him? Aren't you afraid something will happen to him and I'll be lost forever?" I felt tears pour down my face. "Even I'm scared of that. And you act like we are so good for each other, I don't get it."

"Because you are," she said matter of factly. "He is not dying. He is very much alive. He can run, jump, talk, think, laugh, and cry. He's an amazing young man. And you're an amazing young woman," she argued.

"But what if he gets in a car crash and is so hurt he dies?"

"Really?" she asked in an 'I can't believe you just said that' tone. "What if he does? Or better yet, what if *you* get really injured from a piano falling on you?"

"Mom! You know what I mean." I rolled my eyes out of habit, but she couldn't see it in the dark.

"Listen, Brogen, thinking and living as if a piano is going to fall from the sky and kill you any second is no way to live. Jay has to be a little more careful, take medicine, and get checked more often, but there is no guarantee of life for any of us. You and I could die in a car crash tomorrow, and Jay would outlive both of us." She stopped, waited for me to respond, but I didn't. I soaked it in. "And what if he beats the odds and lives way past forty-eight?"

"What odds?" I asked. I didn't recall any odds in our initial conversation. Mom didn't answer right away. I felt a new fear and anger brewing, but needed to be clear I understood what she was saying.

"I guess I forgot to mention that," she muttered, as if she wished she could take it back. "The average life expectancy is forty-eight." I gasped. "But some live longer," she added quickly.

"And some don't," I yelled. "Right? Like his mom." I couldn't believe I hadn't thought about life expectancy. This vEDS stuff seemed so much worse when you put an expiration date on it. "Jeez, could you imagine what it felt like for Jay when they told him he'd be dead by forty-eight?" I was mostly talking out loud to myself. My heart broke for Jay. Life was so unfair. Why did this amazing, beautiful, charismatic, kind guy get this terrible disorder? He's an asset to the human race, not a leech or waste of life. He deserved to grow old, live whatever life he envisioned, have kids, and maybe even grandbabies. "I don't know if I'm strong enough for this, Mom."

She could hear the tears in my voice. She wrapped her arms around me and held me. I lay there in her embrace, thinking about Jay, letting the tears fall quietly. How nice it was to have my mom comfort me. Jay's mom died, and Jay couldn't get a hug from her now when he needed one. I wondered if he got dressed each morning and pondered whether it would be the day he died. Was it the last time he'd tie his shoes, ride a bus, or see a movie? Was he afraid to die? I fell asleep with my mom holding me and endless questions filling my subconscious.

Chapter 17

Things always looked different the next day. Skies seemed bluer, the grass was greener. The worries of yesterday were magically reduced to a manageable size, and brand new ideas and thoughts were born. Oddly enough, Mom's words were like seeds planted in the night, now growing and blossoming inside me. Jay was very much alive. He was healthy, a bit fragile, but more alive than many kids my age who lived life mindlessly. If anything, this stupid disorder made him more alive. Made *me* more alive. I wanted to make memories with Jay— live each day to the fullest, laugh until my belly hurt, cry at sad movies with him, and watch the sunrise and the sunset whenever I could. Life was a gift, not to be taken for granted. It could be here one day and gone the next, or it could go on for a very long time.

My mom had left before I was even awake. I grabbed my phone and texted Jay.

Good luck. I'm thinking about you.

He didn't reply, so I plugged in my phone and got ready for the day. Seconds turned to minutes, minutes to hours, and hours felt like an eternity. I attempted homework, but I was too obsessed with checking my phone. Mom's car finally pulled in the driveway around 4:00 p.m. That was a *long* meeting. No texts or calls. I was like a cat that had been caged all day. I ran to the front door, and Mom seemed weary.

She came up the porch steps. "Hey, sweetie. Let me go change, okay?"

No, I really didn't think I could wait a second longer, but what could I say? I grabbed my phone again to check for a text from Jay, but there was nothing yet. Mom rounded the corner after five minutes wearing sweats, no makeup, and her hair brushed out. She ventured into the kitchen and pulled out the leftover casserole. I stared at her silently, waiting for her report.

She plated up two servings and heated them in the microwave. "Get yourself a drink. We'll chat over dinner."

I obliged and got a glass of tea and poured one for her as well. I sat at the table waiting. Mom placed both plates down and unfolded her napkin in her lap. "You're killing me here. I'm dying to know what happened," I pleaded.

"Okay, well. It was very hard for Jay to tell his dad about vEDS. But he did it." She took a bite of her food.

I was feeling angry, because I could have guessed all of that information on my own. I wanted more specific details. "And?"

Mom cleared her throat and gave me a cautioning look. "Jay has to be the one to tell you most of this, sweetie. His dad heard us out but was very shocked and clearly upset. Time will only tell how he handles the information. I plan to visit with his on-site therapist weekly to advise and check in. If I need to visit him to chat in person, I'll do that." I nodded. Inside I felt thankful my mom cared so much about Jay. "It's going to be hard, for everyone." She continued eating.

"How was Jay afterwards?" I asked. I was surprised I hadn't gotten a text from him yet about his day, or meeting up.

"He was quiet for most of the drive home. He was emotional when he told his dad about it, but then he kind of went inside himself. He probably needs some time to think and let his emotions settle."

I was beginning to doubt that Jay would contact me tonight. I finished dinner with Mom and we talked about plans for the next day. Mom thought it would be a great day to plant some bulbs.

After I cleaned up the plates, I checked my phone. No message. I quickly typed a text to Jay.

Me: Wondering how you are and how it went. Do you still want to see a movie?

Jay: Thanks, I think I need to pass on the movie tonight. Too drained. Catch up with u later.

The ball was in his court. I needed to wait for

him to come to me. I got my running clothes on, and decided I'd go for a run. The evening air was still cool, so I zipped up my hoodie and put on my headphones. Mom saw me stretching in the front hall and knew I was going out for a jog. "I might end up at Meg's, Mom. I'll call if I do." She nodded and waved.

I ran to the school and felt the crisp spring air in my lungs. There was still enough daylight for a short run, so I tried to use the daylight efficiently. I ran countless laps around the school track, feeling the burn in my thighs and calf muscles. It felt good to push my body hard, to feel the muscles grow hard under my skin. The sun began quickly descending and I started to head back. My mind was still thinking about Jay. I felt darkness in me, sadness, like I could feel what he was feeling. Stupid empathic crap. Before I knew it, I realized I was at Jay's house ringing the bell. As I waited for the footsteps from inside to grow louder and open the door, I began to turn and try to flee.

"Brogen. What are you doing here?"

I froze at the sound of Jay's voice. "I'm sorry, I made a mistake. I shouldn't be here."

"Wait, you're already here. What's up?" I studied his face to see if it matched what I felt inside. Unfortunately it did. I could see the sadness in his face and his guarded posture. "Are you okay?" he asked.

"Me? You're asking *me* if I'm okay?" I laughed in a dismissive way. "I…it drove me crazy to think about what you went through today. To not be able to comfort you. Are *you* okay?"

He took a step outside and approached me slowly. "Sorry. Today sucked, but it's over with. I was trying to drown myself in some music and hoped I'd feel better." I turned to face him all the way. He was looking at a crack in the sidewalk. I walked over and wrapped my arms around him. He grabbed hold of me and held onto me as if I could save him. "I hate this," he whispered. "I don't want this fucking disorder. I never asked for it." I could hear the tears in his voice.

"I know." I kissed his cheek. "And I'm so sorry you have to deal with all of this."

He nuzzled in closer. He needed comfort, love, and understanding. He probably needed five years' worth of hugs and love. I rubbed my hand gently along his back.

"You know, even with this news, you are the same Jay you were before the diagnosis. You just have to be a little more careful. Life goes on with no guarantees. People without vEDS can get hit by a car tomorrow and die. So you can't live your life with one foot in the grave."

He looked at me, wiped a tear away, and smiled. "I need to take you to the movies…too much time with you mom. You're starting to sound like her."

"Yeah, I clearly need a better social life."

He laughed. That was a great sign. He sucked in a big breath and let it out. "Thank you."

Our eyes were locked on each other, and I was glad to see he seemed lighter. He took a step closer, closing the space between us so our bodies were touching each other. I felt my heartbeat quicken, and butterflies fluttered about my stomach. This was an intimate space, and he clearly entered it. The air between us changed, it was more electric. He put his hands on each side of my face, and then gently but possessively, he took my mouth against his. He kissed gently at first, and I felt my knees grow weak. His lips were soft, and his breath was hot. I let my mind go and became enveloped in the overwhelming love that Jay exuded. He urged my mouth open and our kiss became more intimate. I felt the heat rising in my cheeks and followed Jay's lead. His hands trailed down my arms and wrapped around my torso. The kisses returned to gentle nibbles, and then to sweet pecks before he pulled away to look at me. All traces of sadness were gone from his face, from inside of me. There was light and love there instead.

"I've been wanting to do that for a long time," he said.

"Well, what took you so long?" I asked and he grinned.

"Life, but I won't let it happen again." He leaned in and gave me a slow, gentle kiss. "I'm picking you up at ten for coffee tomorrow."

"You're not asking, you're telling me?" He nodded with a big smile on his face. "Okay, but only if you come help my mom and me in our garden afterward," I replied. I wasn't sure what he'd say, but I hoped he'd agree to it. Digging in the dirt did wonders for my soul. It cleared my head and centered me. It would be great for Jay.

"Umm, I kinda have a brown thumb." I felt my face fall in disappointment. "But, if it scored me a coffee with you, I'll try," he said. I looked down and realized that at some point Jay had grabbed my hand and was holding it. He followed my eyes and smiled at me.

"Deal, see you around ten." I went up on my toes and gave Jay a quick peck before releasing his hand and waving bye. He returned the wave and put his hands in his pockets as I began jogging home. I made it home in record time to find Mom relaxing on the couch watching TV.

"You never called. Did you stop at Meg's?"

Shoot. "Sorry, actually, I stopped at Jay's. I should have called," I answered.

"Next time call, okay? Did he say anything?"

"He said it was hard. He was pretty upset." Mom listened with her therapist ears, noting my comments in her head. "But then I laid a couple of Dr. Mom lines on him and..." I wondered if I should tell the next part. He'd be here tomorrow, and I really didn't want to hide anything from Mom. "We kissed." Her eyes grew big. She waited for more details, but I wasn't giving any more.

"Just, take things slow, please. Jay's dealing with a lot," she said.

"Oh, I'm in no hurry to speed through this relationship," I replied.

I kissed Mom goodnight and went to my room to text Meg.

Me: Jay kissed me.

Meg: SHUT UP!

Me: Nope, it's true.

Meg: About. Frickin'. Time.

Me: Lol, love you.

Meg: Love you too

I changed into my bedtime clothes and sketched in my journal. Mom peeked in and said goodnight to me. I turned out the light and pulled up the covers. I lay awake thinking about the kiss Jay and I shared. It was beautiful. It meant so much more than if it had happened after a first date. This kiss was spontaneous and filled with love. Magical. My phone beeped and lit up my room. I unlocked my screen and saw a text from Jay.

Jay: Can't stop thinking about you. Goodnight.

I turned to mush inside.

Me: Me too. I'm glad I stopped by. Goodnight.

Jay: XXooo

Me: XXOo

Chapter 18

The next day, Jay picked me up for coffee. We held hands most of the time and kept the conversation light. Even though he didn't kiss me again, it was clear Jay and I had taken a new path in our relationship. True to his word, Jay helped plant bulbs in our garden. He started with gloves on his hands, a gardening apron Mom had in the shed, and tools in hand. He looked like Martha Stewart's apprentice. After several pokes and jabs, I convinced him to lose the gloves—it made for a better gardening experience. He had no idea what he was doing in the garden, but he had a good attitude and did what we advised.

The sun was high in the sky and the day was turning out to be quite warm. "I'll make up some sandwiches while you two finish." Mom walked back into the house and Jay's eyes followed her. As soon as she was out of sight, he leaned over and kissed me. It was the kind of kiss that made time disappear, made you lost in the moment, the kind that poured love from his heart, directly into mine.

We pulled apart, and a sexy grin spread across his face.

"I love your kisses," he said.

I blushed, and then, not knowing how to respond, cleared my throat. "She'll be back any moment. We should finish." Jay chuckled at my awkwardness but finished replacing the mulch over the bulbs. Then we walked to the shed to hang up our tools. I purposely bumped him with my trowel. "Oops, sorry, I didn't see you there." He stopped dead in his tracks and leveled me with his gaze. A few steps more and I bumped him again. "Gosh, I'm so clumsy today."

"Do it again, Brogen, and I'll have to kiss you."

"Is that a threat?" I asked.

"A promise," he said seriously. I laughed at him and then hung up my trowel, took off my gloves, and turned and bumped right into him. "That's it, now you've asked for it," he warned.

"No way. You were ten steps behind me when I went to put the trowel away. You snuck up on me!"

"Doesn't matter how it happened. All that matters is you bumped me again and now I get a kiss."

I swatted his arm playfully, and he stepped on the tips of my toes so I couldn't run away. But once he landed the kiss, there was no more fighting it. I didn't want to be anywhere else in the world.

"Lunch is ready. You two almost done in there?" Mom yelled from the yard.

"Almost," Jay hollered back.

I laughed and he kissed me three more times before grabbing my hand and leading me out to the patio.

***

At school, Jay sat with us at lunch and I enjoyed watching Meg and Jay tease back and forth like brother and sister. Jay always held my hand or placed his hand on my knee during lunch. If we were near each other, we had this magnetic attraction and needed to physically touch the other person. School did not allow many opportunities for private time, but Jay and I had many chances to catch each other's eyes, and there was so much said in those glances. He always walked me home after school and gave me a gentle kiss goodbye.

On one of our walks home, Jay invited me to come over on a Saturday afternoon to watch a movie in his aunt and uncle's basement. Their basement was finished with a leather couch, large flat screen TV, and decked-out stereo equipment. It also had a pool table. Jay said they remodeled it so the kids were more likely to hang out at home than find trouble elsewhere.

Saturday afternoon quickly approached and I put on my comfy jeans and a pale blue henley. I walked down to his house and stopped when I saw Becca's car in the driveway. She and Soren seemed to be getting close, but I didn't trust her. She had it bad for Jay, and I suspected her moves on Soren were to make Jay jealous. Maybe I could call and ask Jay if we could just go to the theater instead. I took my phone out of my pocket and heard the front door open.

"What are you doing out here?" Jay asked.

I pointed at Becca's car. "Is that Becca's?"

"Yeah, but listen, I called the basement. They won't bug us. Besides, I think they're leaving soon."

I felt better thinking they wouldn't be there long. "Okay."

I followed Jay inside. I said hello to his aunt and uncle and glanced around for Soren and Becca but saw no sign of them. Jay told his aunt and uncle we were going to hang out downstairs. He grabbed a few sodas and a bag of chips.

"What are we watching?"

"The Ring. Have you seen it?" I shook my head. "Oh, it's one of the best horror flicks."

I didn't scare easily, so I was up for it. He set our stuff down on the coffee table and got the movie queued up. Then he plopped down in the corner of the couch and motioned for me to sit next to him. I sat close but kept some space between us. He noticed the distance and scooched closer so he could put his arm around me.

"I think I left my purse downstairs." I heard Becca's voice approaching and Jay felt me tense. He squeezed my shoulder to remind me he was right next to me.

"Jay, have you seen my..." Her eyes fell on me. "Well, look who's here."

"Get your purse and go Becca. I think it's by the pool table," Jay said.

"Sorry, was I interrupting your little love fest?"

I rolled my eyes and wanted to shrink away. We didn't need an audience, especially from the peanut gallery.

"Soren! Help Becca get her purse. She's distracted by her need to annoy," Jay shouted up to Soren.

Soren trotted down the stairs. "Hey, Brogen." Soren was always so nice. "Here's your purse. Let's go." Soren grabbed Becca's arm and gave a tug, even though her eyes were still locked on mine. She finally broke the stare and left with him. Soren glanced back at us and Jay saluted a thanks toward him.

"God I hate her," I muttered.

"Seems mutual. What did you do to piss her off?" Jay asked.

"Stole her man."

He smiled and then kissed my head. It made some of my tension leave. He turned and started the movie up. Now, I had seen my share of horror movies, but this one was terrifying. By the end of it, I was in Jay's lap. He had one armed curled around me to protect me, and the other was roaming through my hair and caressing the strands. I honestly did not care what the one hand did as long as one held on tight to me. The movie finally ended and I felt all jumpy and weirded out.

"I thought you said you had some experience with horror movies?" he teased. The TV changed to satellite mode and some action flick showed on the screen. Jay left it on but turned the volume down.

"I did. But who the heck thinks up creepy people coming through TV sets? I'm never going to watch a DVD or VCR tape at home again. Netflix and movie theaters for me." He laughed. "So, have you figured out where you will be this summer? There's only two more months of school."

He let out a puff of air and pondered my question. "I hope I'll be here. I've been thinking about what I'll do when my dad gets out. My aunt and uncle said I can stay with them till college, and I think that is the best plan for now. My dad could use some time to get a job and get used to daily life without the drama of a teenager. I'll visit him on the weekends, but this is a stable house for me to live in while we rebuild our relationship." I nodded. It seemed like a good plan. "And there's this girl who lives close by, and I really want to get to know her. If I move away, I might miss the chance to find out how awesome she really is." He smiled at me and I felt my cheeks blush. He leaned in and kissed me.

"You're pretty awesome yourself," I said with a smile.

He kissed me again, and we spent the next two hours talking, laughing, and kissing. We were two carefree teenagers at that moment. It was the best afternoon I'd ever had. My phone beeped, interrupting our perfect bliss. It was a text from Mom.

Dinner will be ready in 20 minutes. Please be home by then.

"I gotta go." I didn't want to leave. I wanted to spend the rest of forever with Jay. He made me happy. He made me love life.

"I'll text you later. Thanks for spending the day with me." He gave me a peck, took my hand, and led me upstairs. We said a quick goodbye at the door and I left for home. I felt twenty pounds lighter. I had no appetite, too many butterflies filled my stomach, and I could not stop thinking about Jay. At dinner, I knew Mom was talking to me, but I couldn't tell you what she said. I couldn't tell you what I ate. I replayed the afternoon in my head like some lovesick puppy. Jay texted me around 9:00 p.m.

Jay: I'm already missing you.

Me: Me too. What are you doing tomorrow?

Jay: I have a report to finish. Then I thought I might see if this hot babe is home, maybe we could go for a walk in the late afternoon.

Me: You have a girlfriend? Here I thought you were single.

Jay: You're joking right? YOU are the hot babe.

Me: ;> I hoped so, glad you confirmed it.

Jay: So, see you tomorrow.

Me: Can't wait.

***

Jay picked me up around 4:00 p.m. the next day.

"So, Soren and Becca…are they together now?" I asked. Jay shrugged. "I mean, I keep seeing them together."

"I'm okay if they are together, at least then she won't bug me. I don't think Soren is too serious though, he's just havin' fun," Jay said.

"You don't worry she's using him to make you jealous?"

"If she is, it's failing. Besides, if she's preoccupied with Soren, she'll have less time to annoy us." I hadn't considered that, but it made sense. "So, what's the deal with your parents? Divorced?" he asked.

"Yeah, several years ago. Guess some hottie caught my dad's eye, and poor Mom didn't stand a chance. He's actually dating Becca's mom right now."

"Ha! You're joking." He studied my face. "Okay, maybe not…small world." I nodded in annoyed agreement. "So do you see him often?"

"No, and I couldn't care less. I lost all respect for him when he cheated on my mom."

"Your mom's pretty great. He's an idiot to have thrown away a future with her and his daughter." He grabbed my hand and led me toward the bank of the creek. Jay searched around and collected a bunch of different rocks and gave me a small stash of them. We sat on a decaying tree trunk and flung rocks across the gentle creek surface. "I'm sorry about your parents," Jay said as he flung a rock across the water. I thought he might begin telling me more about his parents, but he didn't. He focused on the creek and the rocks.

"Did your parents get along?" I asked. He nodded. "It must have been hard when your mom died. I'm sorry you had to deal with that."

"Thanks. It was pretty hard. Mom was the rock of the family—she supported, loved, and cared for us. And then she went to pull out a meatloaf for supper, and she was gone." My hand covered my mouth, hoping to keep my emotions silenced. I leaned my head against his shoulder in a showing of support. "I wonder if she would have lived longer if the doctors diagnosed her early on in life. Would she have made different choices? Would it have mattered?"

"I don't know. I would hope so. I mean, with your gift of knowledge, you can make different choices. Surely that has to affect the odds," I offered. He nodded. "I wonder if the life expectancy is greater for those that learn about vEDS at a young age."

Jay shook his head. "Honestly, it's a crap shot. I can do everything perfect and still die early, or maybe live super long. Some of it depends on how much crappy collagen is floating around in me. My collagen quality control center has a bunch of idiots, so I have good and bad floating around. So, no guarantees." Jay threw a rock as far as he could. It landed down a ways with a big *plop*.

"So you got your medic alert bracelet. What else do you need to do?"

"Umm, not sure really. I know there's a list of dangerous things to avoid. Rollercoasters, cannonballs in the pool, contact sports…" He stared off into space, taking a moment to mourn the things he had to let go of to 'live more carefully.'

"But you've been on a rollercoaster before, and you clearly you didn't die. I don't get it," I said.

"The stress of the high blood pressure through my arteries can cause an aneurysm to form. Rollercoasters increase blood pressure."

"Well, what about the cannonballs? They don't increase your blood pressure, do they?"

"Nah, no cannonballs for the same reason no contact sports. Chance of rupturing organs from the impact."

"Holy crap. And no surgery?"

"Only if it's to save my life, and they have to be prepared for anything going into it. I guess a lot of people have died during surgery because their body freaks out and turns the tissues to mush. The doctors weren't prepared for that."

"I guess knowing you have vEDS helps prevent that from happening. The doctors can be prepared."

"It still takes someone knowledgeable, though. It seems safer to just avoid it." He threw another rock hard and it landed with a big *plop*.

"Have you heard from your dad?" He shook his head. "He probably just needs time to figure it out." I kept my head on his shoulder and felt the warmth of the late afternoon sun on my face. I felt calm and happy. Jay had that effect on me.

Jay kissed my head and then pulled away just enough to look at me. He stared for a few moments and then a smile spread across his face.

"What?" I asked.

"You look…" He studied me for a long moment. "Nah, never mind."

My eyes popped wide open. I anticipated some form of compliment to come out of him. 'You look…beautiful, sexy, sweet, intelligent, peaceful,' or something, but leaving me hanging was torture. I wanted to know how he was going to complete that sentence. "I don't know what I looked like a minute ago, but I *must* look infuriated right now," I said with a giggle. Jay followed suit and laughed. I tickled his side to try and torture the word out of him. "Tell me!"

"I'll never tell," he gasped between laughs. "Good God, stop, I'll pee my pants." But I continued my assault. Jay grabbed my hand and pulled me so I couldn't reach his side anymore. I lost my balance and fell onto his forearm.

"Crap!" He sat up and made a "T" for timeout.

"Ooh, sorry. Are you okay?" We both checked his arm—no blood, but it seemed to hurt.

"Yeah, guess I shouldn't try to evade your attacks. Listen, wanna head back?" Jay stood and extended his hand to help me up. We brushed off our pants and trekked up to the trail that led to our part of town. "So, thanks for coming out with me today. Great day."

"Yeah, it was pretty great."

Our walk home seemed to take half as long as it did on the way out. The banter between us came so easily, and time flew by. Jay stopped before we got to the front steps of my house. He reached up to grab my face for a kiss. I felt the butterflies take flight in my belly, and then I saw a blue and purple collage out of the corner of my eye. I pulled back and grabbed Jay's arm.

"Holy crap! Did I do this to you?" Jay looked at his arm in disgust. "How did it get this bad in ten minutes?"

"Don't worry about it. I'm fine," he said, trying to change the subject.

"Do you want an ice pack or…jeez, I feel awful for…"

"Would you stop? I'm fine," he shouted. He took a deep breath. "Listen, I gotta go." He turned and walked away.

"Jay, I'm sorry." I felt bad for making a big deal out of it, but I hurt him and wanted to care for him. "Jay!" He didn't look back. He kept walking.

"Is everything okay?" Mom peeked her head out the front door.

"I don't know. I think I made Jay mad." Mom gave me a curious look. "I fell against him and he got this huge bruise. I just wanted to help, get him an ice pack or something to make it better." Mom came out and we both stared at Jay's fading figure as he walked home.

"It must be hard for Jay to be a man and be so fragile. He probably feels self-conscious about it. Just give him some time," she suggested.

***

Time…the next week at school sucked. Jay didn't sit by me at lunch. In the halls, he acknowledged me, but in the most minimal way, as if I were an acquaintance. I tried to give him space, tried not to be overbearing. I sent him a single text at the end of each day that read, "Thinking about

150

you." He never replied. As the week went on, I felt like Jay would never come around. I was sad and miserable without him.

I confided in Meg, and she comforted me. "Listen, Brogen, this weekend I got lawn seats to the concert festival. Sun, music, your best friend by your side…it's what the doctor ordered." I knew she was trying to cheer me up.

"Since when did you become a doctor?" I joked. I liked at least half the bands playing, so it promised to be a good time. Friday night, I didn't text Jay. My sadness turned to anger. I was done coming his way. What crime had I committed against him? I cared too much? No more, I was done.

Saturday morning I got ready for the festival. It was an all-day event in the next town over. Meg picked me up in her new used-car. It wasn't the prettiest set of wheels, but it worked and it was clean. The day was beautiful, 80 degrees, and sunny. I wore my cut offs and a black fitted tee. Meg wore her tight shorts and a tank. We slathered on suntan lotion and walked toward the gates. Music was already blaring through the speakers and the amount of people attending was insane. We found a spot high on the hill, caring more about a decent crop of grass than the best view. We also wanted a fair enough distance between us and the mosh pit. Today was a day for sunning with a friend with some great live music, not dodging fists full of mud.

After the first five bands, we decided to grab some grub. Meg went to get us some hotdogs and chips. I stayed and saved our perfect spot on the lawn. The sun was sinking in the sky and the air would cool off soon.

"Please, just ignore her," I heard a girl say. It was a familiar voice. I turned to see Becca walking up the nearby hill with Soren, who was clearly being dragged along. We met eyes. He waved and I returned the wave. What were the chances of bumping into them in a sea of people? I glanced around but did not see Jay. I lay back down on our blanket. I felt the blanket tug slightly from someone situating themselves on it.

"Long line? I hope you remembered the ketchup and relish."

"Sorry, I didn't." It was Jay. My eyes popped open and I sat up.

"What do you want?" I didn't mean to sound so cruel and cold, but I didn't know where we stood. How random of him to plop down next to me when he avoided me all week.

"To say hi," he turned toward the stage, "and sorry for being an idiot. I was so embarrassed by that bruise. I mean, it's not like you tackled me, but my arm looked awful. I didn't know what to do. I just…ran." He peered down at me, but my face was unreadable—blank and listening. "Can we try again? Life kinda sucks without you."

"I need to know, are you gonna run and shutdown every time something gets hard? Because I can't be in that kind of relationship. It hurts too much. I have feelings too, you know? I felt terrible when I saw that bruise, and I just wanted to make it better. All you had to say was 'no thanks, I'm really okay.' Instead you treat me like…like I'm your enemy."

He was quiet, taking my verbal attack. "I'm really sorry. I can't take it back, but I wish I could." He sighed. "I don't want to do it again, but I can't guarantee I won't make another stupid mistake in the future." He was so sincere. Life did suck without Jay.

I leaned forward and kissed him gently, and he let me. "Okay, we can try again," I said. He smiled and kissed me again.

Meg cleared her throat to get our attention, "Hotdog anyone?"

"Hey, Meg, I'll let you both enjoy the night." He stood and brushed off his jeans. "Soren's gonna send a search party if I don't get back soon."

Meg handed me my food and drink. "Geez, I leave you alone for a few minutes and you reconnect with your man?"

"I know. I was shocked to see him. He said sorry for running away from me."

"Well, I'm glad he was not too prideful that he couldn't apologize. That's a good guy there. I'm surprised you didn't invite Jay and Soren to hang with us."

"One word…Becca."

Meg's mouth dropped open. "Of course. Boy, Becca doesn't waste any time moving in for the kill. Too bad, I thought Soren was kinda cute."

That was the first I'd ever heard Meg mention Soren and cute in the same sentence. Meg and I enjoyed our festival food and the last few bands. We ducked out early in the last set to avoid the crowds.

"Ugh, I need a shower," I moaned. "And a soft bed and clean pjs."

Meg laughed. "And water…lots of water. Thanks for going with me, Brogen. Loved seeing my bands with my girl."

I smiled and patted her knee before exiting the car. I took out my keys and went in through the front. Mom must have already been asleep because the downstairs was dark. I took off my dirty sandals and went to the kitchen for some serious rehydration. After three big cupfuls, I continued to the bathroom for a shower. I shoved my dirty clothes down the laundry chute, turned the water as hot as it would go, then let the water relax me and melt the day away.

Sunday was shopping day. Mom and I stocked up on groceries for the week and bought a few plants for the yard. After helping put away the food, I walked out back to put the plants in the ground. Mom began assembling ingredients for tonight's dinner. I watered the new additions to our garden and threw away the empty containers. As I was storing the tools in the shed, I heard my phone chime.

Brogen, this is Soren, Jay is in the hospital. Call me when you can.

My heart began to race. I clicked on Jay's number. After several rings, Soren picked up.

"Brogen?"

I wanted to skip the intros. "Yeah, what's going on? Is he okay?"

"We don't know yet. He's having terrible stomach pains. My mom is having a hard time convincing the nurses and doctors to check him for the vEDS stuff. They're convinced it's just bad gas or constipation, but I've never seen him like this. He's throwing up and he's pale."

"Can I come up there?" I didn't want to intrude on family stuff, but I honestly wanted to be there for Jay.

"I think that's fine. I'm actually going to swing by the house and pick up the paperwork we got from the genetics office. I can give you a ride."

"Okay, thanks. See you in a few." I hung up and then ran inside.

"Mom, Jay's in the hospital. Soren is going to drive me there in a few minutes." I bolted up the stairs to change clothes and grab a few items to shove in my backpack in case I was there awhile. Mom appeared at my door mid-packing.

"What happened?" she asked nervously.

"I don't know yet. He is having terrible stomach pains and puking. They are trying to convince the hospital staff to see if it's related to the vEDS stuff. Soren said the doctors are not listening and are treating him like he has the common type of EDS, the one that has lots of arthritis."

Mom rolled her eyes in frustration. "I read that it's mishandled often because they think vEDS is EDS. But it's so different. He needs to get scanned for internal bleeding. Make sure they do that. And give Jay a hug from me. I'll try to get up there soon." Soren beeped his horn and I kissed my mom before bounding out the door.

In the car, Soren's leg was bouncing a mile a minute. "Hey, Brogen, ready?" I nodded. "My mom just called. They took Jay back into surgery. Something about a tear in his colon." Soren loved Jay like a brother; there was so much concern in his voice. I was glad Jay had family that had not abandoned him when his life got complicated.

"Surgery? Jay said they only did that as a last resort, and many don't survive surgery. What happened?" I couldn't look at Soren. I was trying hard not to cry. I was so worried for Jay, and if I looked his way, I knew the tears would fall.

"He woke up around six this morning and was in so much pain. We were trying different things at home in case it was gas. But it seemed to be getting worse. Then he started puking, so we headed to the hospital."

All I could envision was Jay in the operating room, lying helpless with tubes coming out from all over. I tried to erase it with thoughts of us tossing rocks into the water and laughing that one afternoon, but the image of Jay on the operating table was stronger. I hadn't realized we arrived at the hospital OR waiting room because I was so lost in my thoughts.

"Brogen, sweetie." Soren's mom ran up to me and hugged me. His dad glanced up with a half smile to greet me. "I hate this stupid disorder." She was crying. I could hear it in her voice and feel my shoulder growing wet. "He's such a sweet kid, why does he have to endure all of this?" I felt a tear slip from my eye. Soren sat down next to his dad and ran both hands through his hair in frustration.

"When will they be done?" I asked.

"They'll let us know, but they expect three hours if there are no complications."

"Would you excuse me? I need a moment." I excused myself and headed to the bathroom. I didn't actually have to use the bathroom, I just wanted some privacy. While in there, I Googled vEDS and colon. Only a few pages came up. I clicked on the first link—it talked about hollow organs being fragile, colons tearing, people often not surviving the surgery, and those who did had to wear a colostomy bag. Now the tears were falling endlessly from my eyes. I could lose Jay. I may have missed my chance to say goodbye. I stood and walked back toward Soren and his family, but I never made it there. Instead, I found myself in the hospital chapel. Strange, since I wasn't even a church going person. It was beautiful, with its warm, ornate wood and stained glass. Candles lit up the front of the chapel. I walked to the front and lit one. And then I said the first prayer I'd ever said in my life.

Dear God, I probably have no right coming to you now in my life. Honestly, I don't even know if you exist. But, if you do, and if miracles exist...one is needed. You see, there is an amazing human being who has gotten the short stick every single time. But he always finds a way to be happy about it, and he makes everyone around him love life. He needs healing. He needs to make it through this. He deserves to live. Please, please help him. Amen.

I sat in the chapel and read more on vEDS. I hadn't researched it since first talking to my mom. I was haunted by all the young faces of those who appeared completely healthy and then suddenly died. They all looked related to Jay—big eyes, straight hair, shadows under the eyes. There was a link to a YouTube video, *Coming Unglued*. I clicked the link with the volume off. It was the saddest four minutes of my life. I watched a man who was being treated for aneurysms in the hospital and was diagnosed with vEDS. His wife gave birth while he recovered from surgery, and he got to meet his newborn son. A few weeks later the dad died, and the newborn son was diagnosed with vEDS. I felt arms around me, and I buried my head in the shoulder holding me while I let the sobs rack my body.

Chapter 19

A lot can happen in six hours. You can get married, buy a car, buy a house, fly to Cancun, have a baby, or die. Jay and I were in the same building, near some of the same people, but our six hours were vastly different. Jay fought for his life, as much as an unconscious person can actually fight. But I believe his spirit, his inner strength, was what warred on. I spent my six hours falling to pieces, grieving for Jay and the countless people who shared his disorder, and getting so angry at how unfair life felt. Meg had turned up in the chapel and found me at my lowest. She's like a sister to me, and she was there to support me when I needed her most.

"Your mom wants to head home once Jay is out of recovery. She'll take me home, and I'm gonna leave my car with you so you can come and go as you need." I hugged her tight. Words were not enough for how much I loved her and how grateful I was.

The three hour surgery had lasted far longer than

anticipated. When the doctors tried to patch Jay, his tissues did not respond like a normal person's. The surgeon came out and told us he was not sure what else to do for him. Jay's tissues were like wet toilet paper, falling apart as they tried to stitch them together. Thank God Mom had showed up at the hospital. She insisted I join a support group through Facebook. Instantly, I was messaged by so many people from around the world who were dealing with vEDS or had a loved one with it. One woman had lost her son to it, and she private messaged me a phone number to a scientist who had years of experience with Connective Tissue Disorders. The scientist's name was Nazli. I called the number given and Nazli spoke with the surgeons and advised them on techniques and materials that have worked in past vEDS surgeries. This one woman's advice helped save Jay's life. For that I would forever be grateful.

"How are you doing, kiddo?" My mom stepped away from Jay's aunt to give me a hug.

"Emotionally fried. But relieved he's gonna be okay."

"You should keep in touch with those people on that Facebook page. Seems like they are an incredible resource and an amazingly supportive group. Jay should join too." I agreed. My phone was pinging like crazy from the Facebook group members. They all wanted to hear the outcome, not to be nosey, but because another person surviving a traumatic event is another positive in their world.

"If Jay's family is okay with it, I'd like to spend the night," I said to Mom, and she nodded. She knew it was a school night, but staying by Jay's side as he healed would do more for me than a day in classes.

Soren and his dad came out of a set of double doors, followed by a gurney carrying a sleepy-looking Jay. The muscles in my face protested as I inverted the frown into a smile that spread across my face. He caught my eye and a little smile lit up his face.

"I'll see you later, pumpkin. Be home by dinner tomorrow, and call me if you need me." Mom kissed my cheek.

"I love you, Mom." I hugged her tight. Then I thanked Meg and hugged her as well. I wanted to let Jay's family visit with him first, so I asked the nurse at the nurses' station where the soda machine was. She pointed down the hall and around the corner. I headed that direction and felt so much lighter knowing Jay had made it through.

"Brogen! Wait—Jay is demanding to see you." Soren was smiling.

I turned and hurried back to the room. Jay's aunt and uncle wore grateful smiles on their faces, and Jay was propped up in bed. He smiled and motioned for me to come closer. I sat in a chair near his bed. He extended his palm for me to take and I wrapped my hand in his.

"We'll give you two a few minutes, guess we can grab some cafeteria food," his aunt said. "Be back in half an hour." She kissed Jay on the head.

"Thanks, Auntie. Love you," he said. She beamed at his words. As soon as they left, he faced me. "Scary stuff, huh?" I nodded, afraid that talking would bring on a new round of tears. "You don't have to stick around. I mean, I'd understand if this was too much for you to deal with." Now the tears were forming in my eyes. He looked away and let go of my hand. "Thanks for helping my family, for helping me. I'm so grateful." He was looking down at his hands.

I knew I needed to coax the words from my mouth, but I was having trouble. I needed to say it the right way. But the words didn't come, at least not right away. I gave up trying to make it right and began spewing what was on my mind.

"I thought you were gonna die. I was so scared. It's so messed up." I met his gaze and he was looking at me with watery eyes. I grabbed his hand and put my hand around his. "But that doesn't change how I feel about you. You are the most beautiful and amazing person I have ever met. Even if you died tomorrow, I would be the luckiest girl for knowing you as long as I did. This vEDS stuff is scary, so scary. But you're not dying, you are not handicapped, you can run, jump, swim, go to movies, ride a Ferris wheel, graduate from college...you still have a lot of living to do." I paused, and he was listening intently. "The scariest thing about all of this is realizing how much I love you. How I want to laugh, cry, and scream at the world with you. Whatever each day brings, I want to live it with you in my life." I unzipped my backpack and pulled out my journal. "My life has changed into something far more beautiful with you in it."

"What's this?" Jay picked up my journal and

opened it to the first page. I explained how I would sketch after each day to release the pressure or energy.

"Look at the dates."

He had made to the part where the images had color. "What changed here? Decided to use color suddenly?"

"I didn't consciously choose to draw in color. That was the day things began to change in our relationship. I sit at the same desk with the same jar of pencils to pick from. You've changed something in me, Jay. It's all right here, proof that my life is better with you in it."

A tear fell down his face. "You're an amazing artist." He pulled on my hand to tug me close. I thought he was going to kiss me, but instead he whispered against my cheek, "I love you too, Brogen." Then he kissed my cheek gently. There was a throat clearing coming from the doorway, so we broke apart and turned to see who was there.

"My turn," Soren said.

"What, you wantin' a kiss too?" Jay puckered up and Soren laughed.

"Yeah, my lips are lonely now that I kicked Becca to the curb."

I couldn't help asking, "*What?* What happened?"

"She overheard me talking to my mom about Jay's vEDS and blabbed it to one of her buddies. Turns out her buddy turned around and told me about it. She's not a keeper. Sorry she spilled the beans, man," Soren said.

Jay returned, "Oh well."

"Hey, Brogen. Mind slipping me Meg's number

before I leave tonight?" Soren asked.

Jay and I both looked at each other, surprised to hear this.

"Sure. Listen, I'm gonna grab a soda and let you guys talk." I kissed Jay on the head and stood to leave. I turned back and studied Jay for a long moment. "By the way, Jay? You look…" I paused, pretending to be deep in thought, and to make the moment more dramatic and nerve-racking. "Nah, never mind." I smiled and walked away.

"Ugh!" Jay's frustrated sound echoed into the hallway and was music to my ears.

Epilogue

Jay

"Brogen, are you ready to go?" I finished tying my shoes, but this simple task seemed overwhelming. The last time I saw my dad was at our wedding. Brogen thought we should invite him, even though he hadn't been in my life since rehab. It was uncomfortable being around him, and my nerves tend to get the best of me.

"I'm ready. Quit being so nervous. You know we won't be alone with him."

Thankfully, my aunt and uncle made an excuse to join us because they 'hadn't seen us in a while.' It was a fib; they saw us every Sunday for dinner, and sometimes during the week. They loved me as if I were their own child, and wanted to support me when I broke this news to my dad.

"You know, we could just send him an announcement." I hoped she would see my humor and agree. Instead, she leveled me with her gaze. This was important to her, so I needed to man up.

"You're lucky I'm so smitten with you that you can manipulate me to do your bidding." I had more of a backbone before Brogen, but love does funny things to you.

"I love you. Everything will be fine, and nothing he says can change the outcome." She kissed my cheek before grabbing her purse.

Brogen and I were expecting a beautiful baby boy in three months. There was still no cure for vEDS, but they had several treatments I had started to try to keep the complications away. Besides the colon tear I had in high school, I made it through the colostomy bag reversal without any problems. My scars were awful, but it was better than having to deal with the bag. Nothing else besides bumps, bruises, and some wicked cuts. Several of our friends on the Facebook support page had passed. Each hurt as if we lost a family member, and a little hope died with each one. They were all "healthy" and died suddenly. Others we knew were dealing with dysautonomic symptoms—including their body not moving their stomach contents—some were in hospice and planning their own funerals, and others were living happy lives past their forty-eight year expiration. It was such a crap shot. Brogen helped me keep my head on and look just two steps in front of me.

"Let's get it over with." I stood and opened the door to the apartment for Brogen. When the sun shined on her face, she looked radiant. The pregnancy made her cheeks flush more often. She was so beautiful, and she was mine. The baby she carried was a symbol of our love for each other.

Brogen had been trying to get me on board with having a baby for over a year. She hadn't convinced me—with a 50 percent chance of giving vEDS to my kids, I couldn't live with myself if I knowingly passed this to my child. I couldn't watch them deal with it. Then Brogen chatted with one of our Facebook support friends who did a procedure called PGD—preimplantation genetic diagnosis. They could identify if the fertilized eggs had vEDS and only implant the ones that didn't. When she suggested we try it, I agreed. Our friends and family supported us, but strangers who didn't know the horrors of this disorder chided us and said we were "wrong to play God." We no longer shared with strangers and acquaintances…not worth the hassle.

The drive across town only took twenty minutes, and my hands felt sweaty. "So if I say 'I think we should get milk on the way home,' that's the signal it's time to leave." When I married Brogen, I started going to a new therapist. She had me create an escape plan to feel more at ease with telling my dad. Brogen had a hard time understanding why I felt this way. Even though he hadn't been in my life, he was still my dad. I still loved him, and I still hoped he'd be happy for me. But I feared the news would unsettle him. He knew vEDS was hereditary, and the news was sure to make him worry his grandchild might have this terrible disorder.

Brogen rang the doorbell, and I wrapped my arms around her, splaying my hands across her growing baby bump. I could do this. I had my girl and my baby. My dad opened the door. He looked from me to Brogen, to Brogen's large belly, then he

rushed out to embrace us.
    "Hi, Dad."

The End

Vascular Ehlers-Danlos Syndrome (vEDS)

The estimated prevalence of vEDS is 1 in 50,000 to 1 in 100,000.

This is not a brand new disorder. A German physician named Georg Sack first recognized it in 1936 and he named it Status Dysvascularis. Since then, other names have been used to describe it: Familial Acrogeria, Sack-Barabas Syndrome, Ehlers-Danlos Syndrome, type IV and/or vascular type. More recently it has come to be known as: Vascular Ehlers-Danlos Syndrome (vEDS).

Vascular Ehlers-Danlos Syndrome (vEDS) is a dominantly inherited, life-threatening connective tissue disorder which results from mutations in the COL3A1 gene. This gene controls the production and assembly of type III collagen. Collagen is the most abundant protein found throughout the entire body. This is what gives connective tissues its strong structural support that acts like cellular "glue" that strengthens and holds your entire body together. Mutations on this gene results in structural dysfunction of the collagen bundles within the connective tissues at the molecular level. These types of mutations cause weakness and fragility to internal organs (GI tract, lungs, liver, spleen, kidneys, bowel/colon, bladder and uterus), arteries and veins that are rich in type III collagen.

Diagnostic Criteria for Vascular EDS
(vEDS – old type IV) include:

Major diagnostic criteria:
-Thin, translucent skin (especially noticeable on the chest/abdomen)

-Easy bruising (spontaneous or with minimal trauma)

-Characteristic facial appearance (thin lips, philtrum, small chin, thin nose, large eyes)

-Arterial rupture

-Intestinal rupture

-Uterine rupture during pregnancy

-Family history, sudden death in (a) close relative(s)

Minor diagnostic criteria:
-Acrogeria (an aged appearance to the extremities, particularly the hands)

-Arteriovenous carotid-cavernous sinus fistula

-Hypermobility of small joints

-Tendon/muscle rupture

-Early-onset varicose veins

-Arteriovenous, carotid-cavernous sinus fistula

-Pneumothorax/pneumohemothorax

-Chronic joint subluxations/dislocations

-Congenital dislocation of the hips

-Talipes equinovarus (clubfoot)

-Gingival recession

Another unofficial minor criteria: which is a common finding in those with Vascular EDS -

They often sleep with their eyelids partially open. (This may also occur in other types of EDS as well)

Note: The presence of any two or more of the major criteria is highly indicative of the diagnosis, and laboratory testing is strongly recommended.

Learn more: edstoday.org

www.annabelleschallenge.org/vascular-eds/

***

vEDS can be diagnosed via blood test or skin biopsy.

Advice I have for those just being diagnosed with vEDS:

-Get and wear a medic alert bracelet stating Vascular Ehlers Danlos

-Know the best hospital to get care from in an emergency (it's often a teaching hospital, or one that can handle rare disorders)

-Educate family, school staff, and your local doctors about vEDS. Because it is rare, you will need to learn about it and advocate for yourself

-Get regular echos, CT scans or MRIs, as well as see your general practitioner regularly

-Inquire about starting one of the medications that have been useful in preventing aneurysms in other connective tissue disorders

-Avoid activities and things that can cause hollow organ rupture or aneurysms

-Avoid elective surgery

-See the top doctors in this field and develop a relationship with them (in the U.S., I recommend

Dr. Hal Dietz and Dr. James Black at Johns Hopkins). These docs can advise your local physicians on how to care for you
 -Make a lot of memories
 -Raise money for research

There is hope!

Researchers have found that several medicines have helped prevent aneurysms in closely related connective tissue disorders such as Marfan's Syndrome and Loeys-Dietz Syndrome. The medicines do this by keeping the blood pressure low (less strain on the arteries) and also by acting on a protein matrix that affects the collagen. This is not a cure, but it is a positive step forward.

Donations for EDS & vEDS research can be made at:

http://www.ehlersdanlosnetwork.org/donations.html

Acknowledgements

I want to thank my husband for holding me up when I was overwhelmed and for his constant support and undying love. You're amazing!

-My mom and her amazing friends for their support and donations to this rare cause.

-Nazli McDonnell for allowing me to add your character at an important part of the story and for being the outstanding scientist and caregiver that you are.

-Dr. Hal Dietz and Dr. James Black for saving so many lives and working hard for a brighter future for vEDSers

-Lynn Sanders for creating an organization, EDS C.A.R.E.S. Network, that donates all of its money toward research.

-EDNF for providing such amazing literature to educate families and physicians about Ehlers Danlos Syndrome.

-Maria for helping me get to this point in my career (and your amazing support – love you!)

-Soren because you color my world and I love you so dearly.

-My editor, for willingly taking on one of my tales, and finding my errors.

Special thanks to Cathy Bowen for providing guidance and love, as well as the information and photo/poster about vEDS at the back of this book which was taken from: EDS Nosology.

http://www.ednf.org/nosology

http://www.genetikzentrum.ch/view/userfiles/files/
Diagnostic_Criteria_EDS_IV(1).pdf

http://www.ncbi.nlm.nih.gov/books/NBK1494/

COL3A1 collagen, type III, alpha 1
http://www.ncbi.nlm.nih.gov/gene/1281

(Superti-Furga et al. 1992)
http://www.ncbi.nlm.nih.gov/pubmed/1506129
http://www.en.wikipedia.org/wiki/Sack-
Barabas_syndrome

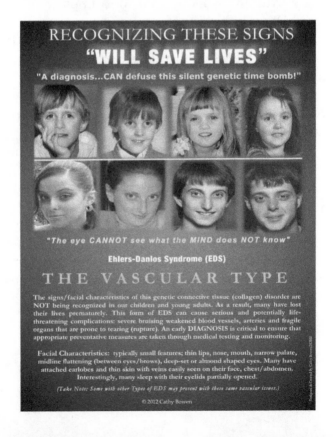

About the Author

D.A. Roach has been telling stories since she was a young girl in the suburbs of Chicago. In college she met the man of her dreams, her happily ever after, and married him 2 weeks after graduating. They have 3 kids together and a pet cockatiel named Gimli. D.A. did not find a love for books until after college. Her parents were immigrants from Lithuania and found tv and radio easier ways to hear stories so they did not do much reading or encourage it. But once she finished college and D.A. had free time, she discovered how amazing it was to get lost in a story.

D.A. is a full time mom and wife. When she is not doing domestic things (laundry, bills, etc) she is writing, reading, creating mixed media art, and helping beautify her kids' school landscape. Oh, and she is ALWAYS listening to music. Her favorite authors include Rebecca Donovan, Richelle Mead, Larissa Ione, Stephanie Meyer, E.L. James, and Sylvia Day. Reading great works from authors like these has motivated D.A. to write her own stories. She hopes to make positive changes in the world with her art and writing.

"Life isn't about finding yourself. Life is about creating yourself."
~ George Bernard Shaw

Facebook:
https://www.facebook.com/DARoachDA

Twitter:
https://twitter.com/daroach12books

Goodreads:
https://www.goodreads.com/author/show/6880131.
D_A_Roach

Blog:
http://daroachbooks.blogspot.com/

CPSIA information can be obtained
at www.ICGtesting.com
Printed in the USA
LVHW050255180221
679445LV00022B/258